All Hallows Eve

About Heather Graham

Heather Graham has been writing for many years and actually has published nearly 200 titles. So, for this page, we'll concentrate on the Krewe of Hunters.

They include:

Phantom Evil
Heart of Evil
Sacred Evil
The Evil Inside
The Unseen
The Unholy
The Unspoken
The Uninvited
The Night is Watching
The Night is Alive
The Night is Forever
The Cursed
The Hexed
The Betrayed
The Silenced
The Forgotten
The Hidden

Actually, though, Adam Harrison—responsible for putting the Krewe together, first appeared in a book called Haunted. He also appeared in Nightwalker and has walk-ons in a few other books. For more ghostly novels, readers might enjoy the Flynn Brothers Trilogy—Deadly Night, Deadly Harvest, and Deadly Gift, or the Key West Trilogy—Ghost Moon, Ghost Shadow, and Ghost Night.

The Vampire Series (now under Heather Graham/ previously Shannon Drake) Beneath a Blood Red Moon, When Darkness Falls, Deep Midnight, Realm of Shadows, The Awakening, Dead by Dusk, Blood Red, Kiss of Darkness, and From Dust to Dust.

For more info, please visit her web page, http://www.theoriginalheathergraham.com or stop by on Facebook.

All Hallows Eve

A Krewe of Hunters Novella

By Heather Graham

1001 Dark Nights

EVIL EYE
CONCEPTS

Sign up for the 1001 Dark Nights Newsletter
and be entered to win a Tiffany Key necklace.

There's a contest every month!

Go to www.1001DarkNights.com to subscribe.

As a bonus, all newsletter subscribers will receive a free
1001 Dark Nights story
The First Night
by Lexi Blake & M.J. Rose

One Thousand and One Dark Nights

Once upon a time, in the future…

*I was a student fascinated with stories and learning.
I studied philosophy, poetry, history, the occult, and
the art and science of love and magic. I had a vast
library at my father's home and collected thousands
of volumes of fantastic tales.*

*I learned all about ancient races and bygone
times. About myths and legends and dreams of all
people through the millennium. And the more I read
the stronger my imagination grew until I discovered
that I was able to travel into the stories… to actually
become part of them.*

*I wish I could say that I listened to my teacher
and respected my gift, as I ought to have. If I had, I
would not be telling you this tale now.
But I was foolhardy and confused, showing off
with bravery.*

*One afternoon, curious about the myth of the
Arabian Nights, I traveled back to ancient Persia to
see for myself if it was true that every day Shahryar
(Persian: شهريار, "king") married a new virgin, and then
sent yesterday's wife to be beheaded. It was written
and I had read, that by the time he met Scheherazade,
the vizier's daughter, he'd killed one thousand
women.*

*Something went wrong with my efforts. I arrived
in the midst of the story and somehow exchanged
places with Scheherazade — a phenomena that had
never occurred before and that still to this day, I
cannot explain.*

Now I am trapped in that ancient past. I have taken on Scheherazade's life and the only way I can protect myself and stay alive is to do what she did to protect herself and stay alive.

Every night the King calls for me and listens as I spin tales. And when the evening ends and dawn breaks, I stop at a point that leaves him breathless and yearning for more. And so the King spares my life for one more day, so that he might hear the rest of my dark tale.

As soon as I finish a story... I begin a new one... like the one that you, dear reader, have before you now.

Prologue

Come to me. Please, come to me.

The words seemed real to Elyssa Adair, like a whisper in her mind, as she looked up at the old mansion.

The Mayberry Mortuary was decked out in a fantastic Halloween décor, customary each year starting October 1. It sat high on a jagged bluff near the waterfront in Salem, Massachusetts. Just driving toward it, at night, was like being in a horror movie. Dense trees lined the paved drive and it was surrounded by a graveyard. The old Colonial building, when captured beneath the moonlight, seemed to rise from the earth in true Gothic splendor.

She shivered and looked around at her friends, wondering if the words had been spoken by one of them. Vickie Thornton and Barry Tyler sat in the backseat, laughing with one another and making scary faces. Nate Fox was driving, his dark eyes intent on the road.

No one in the car had spoken to her.

She gave herself a silent mental shake. She could have sworn she'd actually heard a whisper. Clear as day. *Come to me.* Strangely, she wasn't afraid. She loved the artistry of Halloween—the fun of it—and few places in the world embraced the day like Salem.

This was home and she loved Salem, despite the sad history of witch trials and executions. A lot of that was steeped in lure and myth, but the local Peabody Essex museum and other historic venues seemed to go out of their way to remind visitors of the horror that came from petty jealousy and irrational fear.

"Boo," Nate said, leaning toward her.

She jumped with a start.

She'd been deeply involved in her thoughts and the view of the old mansion. Nate, Vickie, and Barry all giggled at her surprise.

"Do you have to do that," she murmured.

He frowned, his eyes back on the road. "Elyssa, we've done this every year since we were kids. So are you really scared now?"

"Of course not," she said, and tried to smile.

She loved Nate. They were both just eighteen, but they'd been seeing one another since their freshman year. She was young, as everyone kept reminding her, but she knew that she would love him all of her life. Despite them being opposites. She was a bookworm, born and raised in the East, red hair and green eyes. He was from South Dakota, a Western boy, whose mom had been from nearby Marblehead but whose dad had been a half Lakota Sioux. He was tall and dark with fabulous cheekbones and a keen sense of ethics and justice. He was their high school's quarterback, and she was debate team captain.

"Don't be silly," she said. "Last year, I played a zombie, remember?"

And what a role. She'd arose from the embalming table and attacked one of her classmates who'd played the mortician, terrifying the audience.

Nate grinned. "That you did. And what a lovely zombie you were."

Please.

She heard the single word and realized no one in the car had spoken it. Instead, it had vocalized only in her mind. Incredibly, she managed not to react. Instead, she pointed out the windshield and said, "Looks like someone has decided to toilet-paper the gates."

White streamers decorated the old wrought iron, which seemed original. Time had taken its toll on both the gates and the stone wall that had once surrounded the property. She'd never minded that such an historic property was transformed each year into one of the best haunted houses in New England. And despite the decorations, the house remained open daily until 3:00 P.M. for tours. It had been built soon after Roger Conant—the founder of Salem—moved to the area, around 1626, starting out as a one-room building. Nearly four hundred years of additions had blossomed it into a spacious mansion, the last editions coming way back in the Victorian era. In the early 1800s it had been consecrated as a Catholic church, deconsecrated by the 1830s when a new church had been built closer to town. Some said the site had then been used for satanic worship, taken over by a coven of black magic witches, but she'd never found any real support for those rumors. During the Civil War it served as a mortuary—drastically needed as the torn bodies of Union soldiers returned home. That continued until the 1950s when the VA made it a hospital for a decade. Finally, the Salem Society for Paranormal Studies bought the property. Along with historical tours, it offered tarot card and palm readings and ESP testing of anyone willing to pay the fee. The society had repaired and restored the old place, eventually garnering an historic designation, ensuring its continued preservation.

In the 1970s, Laurie Cabot came and created a place for dozens of modern-day Wiccans, and the area soon become a mecca for everyone and everything occult. Overall, though, the society people were barely noticed, except by fundamentalists who just didn't like anything period. Actually, the Wiccans had brought a great deal of commerce to town, and that was something to be appreciated.

Please, please, come. I need you.

Elyssa didn't move, not even a blink. Now she knew. Those words were only in her head. Maybe she needed sleep. Definitely, she shouldn't drink any more of the cheap wine Nate's brother found at the convenience store.

Last night's overindulgence had been plenty enough.

They drove through the gates and past the graves. Like every other New England cemetery, this one came with elaborate funerary art and plenty of stone symbolism. One angel in particular had always been her favorite. She occupied a pedestal near the drive, commissioned for a Lieutenant Colonel Robert Walker in 1863, there to guard his grave, on one knee, head bowed, weeping, her great wings at rest behind her back.

They drove by and the angel seemed to look up—straight at Elyssa. Again, she heard the words in her head.

Please, help me. Find me.

"Look at the people," Vickie said.

The lines to get inside the haunted house stretched down the main walk to the porch, then around the corner of the house. The mansion was huge—seven thousand square feet over three stories, with a basement and an attic. Creepy windows filled the gables and projected inside dormers from the slate roof, like glowing eyes in the night.

"It's three days before Halloween. What were we expecting?" Nate asked. "This place is popular. But it looks like there are vendors walking by with hot chocolate. We'll have fun in line."

"Elyssa, can't you get us into the VIP line?" Barry asked. "Don't you still have friends here? Didn't they ask you back to work inside the haunted house this year?"

She nodded. "I just couldn't make it happen, not with getting the whole college thing going for next year. But, I'll see what I can do. John Bradbury still manages the place. He's a good guy to work for."

"Don't you know Micah Aldridge too?" Vickie asked. "Isn't he one of the main guys in the paranormal society?"

"He's never around at night. He and that weird, skinny lady from Savannah—Jeannette Mackey—have their noses up in the air at this kind of thing. They think they're a little above all this fun."

They parked far away, almost in the graveyard, and walked back to the line.

"Work your magic," Vickie told her.

Elyssa headed toward the makeshift desk and plywood shelter in the front where Naomi Hardy was working ticket sales. She was surprised to see that she'd been wrong. Micah Aldridge was there, helping with the sales.

Elyssa smiled at Naomi, then leaned down to talk to Micah. "I thought you hated this silliness."

He was a good-looking man who worked his dark hair and lean, bronzed features to add an aura of mystery to his appearance. His usual attire was some kind of a hat and long coat, reminiscent of a vampire, regardless of the season, and tonight was no exception.

"I don't hate what pays the bills," he told her, adding a smile. "Wish you would have worked this year. It's always great to see you."

"I just couldn't, not with college coming up." She drew in a breath. "Micah, I have some friends with me, and we're happy to buy tickets, but we can't afford VIP entrance and the line—"

Her words trailed off and she grimaced.

"Say no more, little one," he said.

To her surprise, he didn't let her pay. Instead, he set a BE BACK IN A MINUTE sign before his seat. He then whispered to Naomi Hardy, a pretty young woman of about twenty-five, who was selling the tickets to each person in line. Naomi was John Bradbury's assistant. She knew Naomi took a room in Salem for the month of October, but lived down in Boston.

Naomi smiled and nodded an understanding, then said, "Enjoy."

Micah led them up to the porch to wait for the next group to enter. She thanked him profusely, but he brought a finger up to his lips, signaling for quiet.

"Not even time for hot chocolate," Vickie noted, smiling.

"We'll get some after," Nate said.

In the mansion foyer they were greeted by a hunchback Igor-like actor who told them a tale about black masses in the house, mad scientists, and more. They then began the walk-through, starting with the dining room where skeletons had gathered together for a feast. One was a live actor who rose to scare each group as they entered. Next came the kitchen—where a cook was busy chopping up human bodies for a stew and offering the visitors a bloody heart.

Staged gore had never bothered Elyssa. She didn't mind the mad experiments in one of the bedrooms, or the Satanists sacrificing a young woman in the tarot card room. She didn't even mind the demented baby or the usual scare-factor pranks typical for haunted houses.

In an upstairs bedroom, they came to the mad scientist's lair where an actor was busy dissecting a woman on the bed, vials, wires, tubes, and beeping machines all around him. The woman—despite the fake gore—looked familiar.

Then she realized.

It was Jeannette Mackey.

Elyssa smiled and kept quiet, but when the rest of her group had filed out, she paused and hurried to the bed.

"What are you doing here?" she asked.

Jeannette grinned at her and replied with her sweet accent. "Darlin', when you can't beat'em, you've got to join'em."

Elyssa laughed, found Jeannette's hand, and squeezed it. "You and Micah working the show and Naomi Hardy on the ticket booth. Did they not get enough kid volunteers this year?"

"Gotta get back to work," Jeannette said. "New group is coming in. But, no, we're doing this just because we love the place."

Elyssa grinned and hurried out.

The other bedrooms on the second floor offered a Satanist mass, a headless tarot card reader, and two displays of movie monsters with ice picks, electric saws, and more scary weapons.

Then it was time to head down—way down.

Elyssa had always been oddly uneasy in the basement. That's where the embalming had once been done, and it hadn't changed much since the days when the house had served as an actual mortuary. The trestle tables were still there. The nooks and crannies where shelves with instruments had been kept remained too. Hoses above stone beds still hung, where real blood and guts had been washed away, the bodies readied for embalming. There was something sad and eerie about the place.

Vickie screamed and gasped delightedly. Barry kept an arm around her—except when he was jumping himself. There were motion-activated creatures in the arched nooks along the way. One, some kind of an alien creature, took Nate by surprise and he leapt back, causing them all to laugh.

But Elyssa's attention had been drawn to another of the basement nooks, a figure of a hanging man. She'd seen the group before them walk right by it—no blood, no gore, no actor to jump at them. To locals the image was nothing new. It could be seen throughout Salem, representative of men like George Burroughs or John Proctor, who'd also been convicted of witchcraft and hanged, like the women, during the craze.

Her head began to pound.

And she was drawn toward the image.

Yes, thank you. Come. Please, help me stop this.

She stared through the darkness and her first thought was how life-like the image was. But, of course, the man had been hanged. He was dead. No life existed. She could see every little hair on his head. He was dressed in Puritan garb, as if a victim of the witch trials. The nook had been painted to look as if it were outside at the hanging tree. He might have been about thirty-five or so in life, with dark hair and weathered features. And the smell. Rank. Like urine and rot. The area had really been done up to haunt all of the senses.

She moved closer.

Yes, yes. Help. Please, oh, yes, please.

The voice whispering in her mind grew louder.

One more step.

And then she knew.

The figure was real. Not an actor there to scare those who came so giddily through the house. And she knew him. He ran this place. He'd even given her a job here at the house last year.

John Bradbury.

Hanging, dead.

She screamed, which only evoked laughter at first. But she kept screaming and pointing. Her friends tried to calm her. Nate tried to show her that it was just part of the scare fest. A prop.

But he suddenly realized that it was much more.

White-faced and grim, he shouted, "That's a real body. He's dead."

The night seemed to drag on forever with the police, bright lights and horrified actors wanting to go home, Mayberry Mortuary haunted house closed down. Eventually, there was hot chocolate as they sat in the mortuary café, answering questions for cop after cop.

But, that wasn't the worse part.

That came when Elyssa finally made it home in the wee hours, lying in her bed, drifting in and out of sleep.

She felt her mattress depress and when she opened her eyes, John Bradbury was there.

Thank you. But you have to know. They're going to kill again, unless you stop them.

Chapter 1

"There?" Sam Hall asked.

"Oh, yes. Yes. Touch me there. Right there," Jenna Duffy moaned in return.

"Right here? I can touch and touch and—"

"Ohhhh yes. That's it."

Jenna rolled over and looked up at him, eyes soft, smile beautiful. He'd been straddled over her spine carefully balancing his weight as he worked his magic. Now he towered over her front.

"I think," she said, reaching up to stroke his cheek, her eyes filled with wonder, "that you missed your calling. The hell with the law. The hell with the FBI. You could have been an amazing masseuse. My shoulders feel so much better."

"You shouldn't spend so many hours reading without taking a break and walking around."

Jenna nodded. "I don't know how Angela does it. She has such an eye for the cases and requests, when we're really needed. I've read them over and over."

She was referring to Special Agent Angela Hawkins, case facilitator for the Krewe of Hunters at their main offices—and wife of Jackson Crow, their acting field director. Both he and Jenna loved their work. When they weren't in the field, he maintained his bar licensing in several states by working Krewe legal matters. Jenna assisted Angela in reading between the lines, determining where the team was most needed. The requests for Krewe help were growing in number; and while new agents came on all the time, it was still a race to keep up.

"We have tomorrow," he said. "Then vacation."

"Sun, sea, and tanning oils for exotic massages," Jenna said, laughing.

He stared down into her eyes—greener than the richest forest—and marveled at the way he loved her. Her hair, a deep and blazing red, spread out across the pillows in waves. It seemed incredible that this remarkable, beautiful, sensual woman could feel the same for him. That they could lie together so naturally, that laughter could combine with passion, and that they could live and work together.

And still be closer each year.

He smiled and kissed her.

Her fingers ran down his spine with a teasing caress, finding his midriff, then venturing lower.

"What are you thinking about?" she asked.

He groaned softly.

"Pardon?"

"Sex. Here, now," he said. "The perfect place. In bed—both of us on it."

She frowned.

"And you weren't?"

She smiled and caressed him in one of her most erotic and sensual ways. "There?" she whispered teasingly.

"Oh, yes. Right there."

"I can touch and touch and touch."

He kissed her lips, then her collarbone and her breast, moving lower. He loved her so much, truly loved her, and every time they made love, it seemed sweeter and sweeter. Her skin was satin, her hair the fall of silk, and her movements—

Those were the best.

They slept after, entangled in one another's arms, and he thought about heading to Atlantis and how he'd planned to ask her then if they shouldn't begin to think about a wedding in the near future.

What a beautiful night.

But in the morning everything changed.

With the phone call.

* * * *

A wickedly big and warty witch atop a broomstick rode above a sign that advertised "Best Halloween Ball Bash in the Nor'East."

New England. Halloween.

Nothing went better together.

And the holiday decorations would just increase as they neared Salem, Massachusetts, the days ticking off closer and closer to the hallowed day. Costume shops abounded, as if they'd sprouted from seeds of alien pods tossed down by a space ship. But people everywhere liked to party.

Unfortunately, this was not going to be a vacation in the Bahamas. Sadly, Sam thought about the tickets he and Jenna had changed and the rooms in the fantasy casino they'd canceled. He didn't mind. If Jenna needed to do something else, that was fine. As long as he was with her.

And he was.

"So," he said, frowning slightly as he glanced over at Jenna before looking back at the road. "Talk to me. We're here to see a relative but, somehow, I never met her when you and I first got together, back with the murders at Lexington House. And, a relative I also haven't met since."

Then again, they hadn't been back to Salem that many times over the past few years. Jenna's parents lived in Boston—when they weren't visiting friends and family in Ireland—so they'd only made it that far when they popped up for a weekend. Her uncle, Jamie O'Neill, her next-favorite relative, often came down to Boston when they were there.

Jenna didn't look at him. She was gnawing her lower lip, staring out the window. She'd grown more and more withdrawn since they'd left Boston's Logan Airport and started driving up US 1 toward Salem. He wasn't sure if she had even heard him.

Salem.

His home.

And while Jenna had come from Ireland as a child and grown up in Boston, her ties with Salem were deep. Her Uncle Jamie lived here, and she'd spent a tremendous amount of time, while growing up, with him. Salem was where he'd fallen in love with Jenna. And when they'd left, he'd assumed he'd open a law practice in northern Virginia. Instead, he'd found himself in the FBI academy.

And then part of the Krewe.

Thing was, though, until the call came, he'd never expected to be heading here. And he'd never expected that she'd close down. Jenna was an experienced agent. She dealt with a lot of bad things. She had a tremendous compassion for others and a stern work ethic. She'd been almost silent as they'd ridden to work, explaining only that they were going to have to change things up. No vacation right now. She'd gotten a call from an Elyssa Adair, someone he'd never heard her mention before. She was sorry, so sorry, about the trip, and she wanted to wait until they saw Jackson before explaining why this was so important. As soon as they'd arrived at work, he'd arranged for them both to speak with Jackson Crow at the Krewe of Hunters special unit headquarters.

He wasn't surprised that Jenna had so quickly been given permission for the two of them to travel to Salem. Krewe cases were often accepted on instinct, or because there was a particular reason a Krewe member should be involved. He was surprised, though, by Jenna, who was usually open and frank and outgoing, especially with him. They'd been together nearly five years. He'd changed his entire life to work with her and, of course, to deal with the fact that the dead seemed to like to speak with him.

And he loved her.

With all of his heart, with everything in him.

He knew that she felt the same way about him, which made it so strange that she'd seemed to shut him out, even while asking that he accompany her and assist on the case. At the moment, however, there wasn't a case. Not one that they'd been invited to join in on at least. A man was dead. He'd been associated with the old Mayberry Mortuary Halloween Horrors. Police were suggesting that he might have killed himself over financial matters. There was an ongoing local investigation. But, so far, the death was being considered a possible-suicide.

That much, he knew.

The minute Jenna had begun to talk about a cousin he'd never met, Elyssa Adair, and the fact that Elyssa had discovered the dead man in the haunted horror attraction, he'd probed for background.

John Bradbury, born in Salem, schooled in Boston, had returned to Salem to operate the mortuary under the business umbrella Hauntings and Hallucinations, Inc. The company was doing fine. However, the year before, Bradbury had gone through a tough divorce, and, apparently, due to past substance abuse problems, had lost all but supervised visitation rights with his three children. His ex-wife—while crying on a newscast—had told the world that it had been John's mental instability that had led to his self-medicating with drugs and alcohol and their subsequent divorce.

This was still New England, and while Sam held his own devotion to his home sector, he was aware that some of the old Puritanical values still hid in the hearts and minds of many. Mental weakness was kept to one's self. Everyone was shocked that the man killed himself, considering how calm he'd appeared to his employees and how happy he'd been when managing the mortuary in its guise as a haunted house. It would be easy to accept the death as an apparent suicide. Bad things happened around Halloween. Holidays seemed an impetus for those dealing with severe depression.

They were passing through Peabody—an old stomping ground for anyone who'd grown up in the area. Beautiful old Colonial and Victorian homes, big and small, grand and not so grand, were decked out in ghostly fashion, all the more eerie as night began to fall. Scarecrows, skeletons, ghosts, ghouls, black cats, and more abounded.

But the best was yet to come.

Salem prided itself on being Halloween central.

Jenna finally turned his way and said, "She's a little scholar. Elyssa was in Europe when we were here last. She earned six months study abroad before she was even a freshman. She's a great kid, a second cousin once removed or however you come about that. My dad's cousin's daughter's daughter. She's all grown up now, a senior and just turned eighteen. She's never seen a dead body—much less a hanged dead body."

Except in museums, probably. Many of Salem's attractions had scenes of life's finales, men and women convicted and executed after their so-called witch trials.

"I can imagine how bad it was," he said.

"She was nearly hysterical on the phone, and, of course, her folks are upset that she called me. They seem to think she's having a bad reaction to what happened. But I told her mom not to worry, that I was happy to come and see Uncle Jamie and that we had some vacation time coming anyway." She paused and looked at him apologetically. "I said I was happy to help her in any way that I can. The thing is—"

Her voice trailed.

He waited.

He knew her dilemma, listening intently when she'd explained the situation to Jackson Crow. Elyssa believed that a dead man had called her for help. Then that same dead man had appeared to her later to thank her for finding him, fading away with a warning that a killer had to be caught before more people died. Elyssa's parents would want Jenna to assure the young girl that what was happening in her mind was because of the horror she'd seen, not because a dead man could really speak to her.

"It's going to be hard," Jenna said. "I can't tell her that she's imagining things if, in fact, she's not. And if this man was really murdered, someone has to discover the truth about his death."

He reached across the car and squeezed her hand. "You'll do what's right. You always do."

She nodded and squeezed back.

They really hadn't talked about this much at all. Instead, they'd left the office, packed, and hopped onto the first plane. Angela had seen to it that a rental car was waiting for them. Normally, she would have seen to it that they had a hotel room too.

But, not in Salem.

Sam still owned a house here. His parents' home, where he'd grown up. Once, he'd wanted to sell the house and say good-bye to Salem. But Jenna and her Uncle Jamie had changed that. He'd learned something about his childhood home because of them, because of all of the bad that had happened.

Three things.

People made bad things happen.

Places weren't evil.

And when the dead remained, it was for a reason, usually to make sure that the living finally got it right.

He entered Salem and drove down Walnut Street, heading into the historic district. People, off to early holiday parties, filled the sidewalks in costume. Around this time of the year it was difficult to tell the practicing Wiccans from all the amateurs.

"How cute," Jenna murmured, noting a group of children, all in costumes themed to *The Wizard of Oz.*

They stood at a stop sign, and Sam took a minute to look at the group and smile. He was about to move through the intersection when he suddenly slammed on the brakes. A costumed pedestrian had rushed into the street and thrown himself on the hood of the car, grinning eerily at them. He stayed for a beat while Sam felt his temper flaring. The person in the costume stared at him through the windshield, donning a red latex mask. It seemed the entire body was red beneath a black cape, the eyes blood-streaked yellow. The person suddenly pushed off the car, cackling with laughter.

"Ass," Sam yelled.

"Total dick," Jenna said.

"Vampire, demon?"

"Boo-hag," Jenna said.

He didn't know about a boo-hag. "What's that?"

"I guess it's a regional thing, from the Gullah people. They're from regions of Africa, mainly brought to this country as slaves. They got together and formed a group hundreds of years ago. They have a language, kind of like a Haitian *patois* joined with English, and all kinds of cultural stuff. And of course now, with time passing, the mix is African, Creole, and so on. They're known to have lived in the low country of South Carolina, down to north Florida at one time."

"And what do these boo-hags do?"

"To the Gullah, there is a soul and a spirit. The soul goes to Heaven, assuming the person was good, the spirit watches over the family. Unless it's a bad spirit. Then, it becomes a boo-hag. Like a spiritual vampire."

"A spiritual vampire?" Sam asked.

She turned to him, grave and knowing, a slight smile in her eyes. "When you slept eight hours and woke exhausted, that might have been a boo-hag. They suck energy out of the living. Usually, they leave their victims alive so they can feast off of them again. If a victim struggles, that's when you find that person dead in the morning."

"And how do you fight a boo-hag?" Sam asked.

"You need to leave a broom by your bed. Boo-hags are easily distracted. They'll start counting the bristles and forget they came to suck your energy. To rid yourself of a boo-hag, though, you have to find their skin while they're out of it, and fill it with salt. That will make them insane with agony when they put it back on."

"Guess we need to sleep with salt and brooms," he said. "Easy enough to find at Halloween. How the hell do you know about all this? This is Salem, Mass, not the Deep South."

"You had to have known my mum's mother. She taught me all about the banshees and leprechauns. She loved legends. And she also had a dear friend from the low country who lived in Charleston."

"Wish I could have known her," Sam said. He was suddenly glad of the obnoxious drunk who'd thrown himself on the car. Jenna had finally become Jenna.

"Those eyes," she said, with a shiver. "Spooky."

"Contacts, most likely."

"Good ones, too. But there are a lot of great costumes at Halloween. You know that."

He did. "And no costume parties, huh?"

She grinned. "No costume parties. But you'd make a great John Proctor. He was supposed to have been a big, tall, strong dude."

"Before he was hanged," he said.

She grimaced at that.

They were nearly in the historic section.

He turned to her sheepishly. "I forgot to ask. My house? Or is Uncle Jamie expecting us?" Sam asked.

She turned to him, more relaxed than she'd been. "Uncle Jamie is expecting us."

"Okay, just so I know where I'm going."

She nodded, and he noticed a darkness settle over her again. There was something so pained about her eyes, and yet there was so much appreciation in them he felt a tug at his heart. He remembered meeting her when Malachi Smith had been accused of the brutal murders at Lexington House, and how strong and determined she'd been. Between her and Jamie, he'd found himself representing the young man pro bono. Even in the height of danger and true horror there, she'd never looked like this.

But this time her family was involved.

"I'm here," he said. "Jamie is here. And you're the best damned agent I know. Things will work out fine."

"Thanks," she said.

He drove to Jamie O'Neill's eighteenth century house, not much different from his parents'. Jamie kept the place in excellent shape. He was an exceptionally good man who'd almost gone into the priesthood. Instead, he'd studied psychiatry and donated an awful lot of pro bono work, always helping the underdog. Sam had known Jamie before he'd returned on the day of the Lexington House murders. He'd even met Jenna, though all he remembered of that day was being called upon by his parents to supervise a group of rowdy teenage girls.

Today, Jamie's house seemed strange as he eased onto the old stone drive in front. Like a dark cloud had settled over it. But the afternoon was waning. Massachusetts's autumns brought night quickly. Still, it seemed to

Sam that clouds sat over the house and nowhere else. Jenna's family was certain that the property was haunted, but by nice ghosts they claimed. Ghosts that went about their business and left the living to their own. He was curious about Elyssa Adair and her family. Apparently, they didn't possess Jenna's mom's and dad's ability to shrug off anything that might be paranormal.

The door opened and he saw Jamie O'Neill step out on the porch. He wore a sweater and jeans, but cast a grave look about him that Sam could not remember seeing often. He lifted a hand in greeting, as Jenna ran up the walk to hug him. Sam opened the trunk of the rental car and grabbed their bags.

A young woman burst from the house behind Jamie. She had red hair, similar to Jenna's. Tall, lean, pretty, upset, yet relieved.

"Jenna. Thank you for coming."

Sam knew that the young lady had to be Elyssa Adair.

"That was never in doubt," Jenna said, engulfed in a tight and enthusiastic hug.

Sam moved forward, setting the bags down as Jenna disentangled herself and turned to make the introductions. "Elyssa, this is Special Agent Sam Hall. We work together and we're together, too."

"Uncle Jamie told me all about that," Elyssa said.

The younger woman stared at him with beautiful eyes that weren't quite as rich a green as Jenna's. Then she threw her arms around him and hugged him.

Withdrawing at last, she said, "I knew you would come, too."

He was puzzled. "Can I ask how?"

"The ghost told me. John Bradbury specifically said you were coming, and that was before Uncle Jamie ever mentioned you. He said he knew you when he was alive."

Chapter 2

"Come in," Uncle Jamie said after greeting Jenna and Sam.

Jenna looked at her uncle anxiously, wondering why she had such a bad feeling about what was going on. Elyssa had calmed and smiled at Jenna.

"Are you all right?" Jenna asked, hands on her young cousin's shoulders. She hadn't seen Elyssa for years, although they kept up on Facebook. Their lack of a visit hadn't been on purpose, just the way life had fallen into place.

"I'm fine," Elyssa said. "Now that you're here."

There was that unshakeable faith Elyssa seemed to have in her. Which was a lot to live up to.

"Let's talk," she said to both Elyssa and her uncle.

For a man who accepted just about anything on earth and maintained his faith with the loyalty of an angel, Uncle Jamie could be very matter-of-fact. "We need to, before Susan gets back."

"Susan?" Sam asked, following Jenna across the porch to the front door.

"Elyssa's mother," Jamie said.

A minute later Uncle Jamie had served them all coffee and they sat around the dining room table. Jenna felt Sam's hand on hers and met the strong gravity in his eyes.

"I'm here," he said softly.

She nodded, a thank you in the squeeze she returned on his hand.

"From the beginning," she told Elyssa. "Tell me everything."

Elyssa glanced nervously at Uncle Jamie, took a breath and began. "Mom says I'm crazy. Dad is looking into 'trauma doctors.' I'm pretty sure he means shrinks." She paused. "Uncle Jamie came to the house. Mom thinks he's almost a priest—and he was almost—so she let me come here and she even said it was okay to talk to you because you're with the FBI. She thinks you'll make me understand the difference between a suicide and a murder. And Uncle Jamie has been the best person in the world for me because he doesn't think that I'm crazy. He seems to believe in...whatever it is."

Jenna thought about how much she really loved her uncle. He told her once that he believed deeply in his faith, so he had to accept that there was life after death. And who was he to declare that departed souls might not linger, trying to help others.

"What makes the police think it was suicide?" Sam asked.

Elyssa flushed uncomfortably. "There was a kicked over stool found near where he was hanging, right in the niche."

Sam shrugged. "Could have been planted."

"Why don't you tell us what happened exactly, from beginning to end?" Jenna said.

"We're open to hearing everything you have to say," Sam added.

Elyssa looked at Sam and nodded. She seemed to have taken an instant liking to him. Unlike Jenna, who'd admired Sam's stature and reputation from the beginning, but had not been all that enamored. It had been Uncle Jamie who'd known that Sam would come around to their way of thinking, and their determination to find the truth about the Lexington House murders. And then she'd been lucky. Sam had fallen in love with her, while she was falling hard for him. And now she couldn't imagine her life without him. It didn't hurt that he really was a gorgeous man, rugged, tall, smooth and dignified, with a rock hard jaw and a steely determination when he made up his mind to get something done.

Elyssa launched into her story. She'd just been out for a night of fun and heard a strange voice in her head, which she ignored. She'd tried to connect with John Bradbury when they'd reached the mortuary, but he'd not been around.

Then she found him.

Hanging dead.

The haunted attraction had been closed down and she'd answered questions over and over again. Back home, her mom had actually made her tea with whiskey in it so that she could sleep. But then she'd opened her eyes and John Bradbury had been sitting at the foot of her bed, telling her that he was grateful, but that she had to stop what was happening or other people would die.

"He didn't by any chance tell you what was happening, did he?" Sam asked.

"He doesn't really know. He was working downstairs in the embalming room when someone slipped a noose around his neck. He heard people talking, two people, he thinks. Then someone said something about the witch trials and wacky cults. Another voice said something about that person needing to shut up. And then the person who'd spoken first said what the hell did it matter? Bradbury would be dead. Who cares."

"The witch *trials*?" Jenna asked, adding, "Not Wiccans today?"

Elyssa nodded. "The witch trials, that's what he said. Someone was talking about the witch trials and cults. But, what they said exactly, I don't know." She looked hopeful. "Maybe now that you're here, John will come and talk to you instead of me. I can't remember all that he said. I'm not sure he knows exactly what he heard."

"We'll look into whatever new groups are in town," Sam said. "And, of course check out the older covens and groups too. Most of the Wiccans in town are good and peaceful people. They practice their faith like any religion."

"Good people come in all faiths," Uncle Jamie said. "Elyssa knows that."

"I mean, that's the thing. I couldn't figure out why he appeared to me. I'm in my last year of high school," Elyssa said. "I have midterms coming up. I'm not the police or even an investigator. Early this morning he came back. He wasn't a creepy ghost or anything. He didn't pop into the shower on me or anything like that. He appeared right when I'd finished dressing. Mom said I shouldn't go to school today. When I first woke up—that's when I called you, Jenna—I was still feeling freaked out. Then you said that you'd come and I was so relieved. I was finally hungry and was going to go out to get some breakfast when he appeared at my bedroom door. He thanked me again and said that you and Sam could help."

Sam smiled at her. "He came back and talked to you in your room and you didn't scream or pass out? Pretty brave kid."

Elyssa smiled. "Maybe I'm like you."

"Maybe you are—and it's really not so bad," Jenna told her.

"Should we have known this man?" Sam asked.

"He was from Salem," Jenna told him. "Five to ten years older than you. Do you remember his name from anything?"

Sam reflected for a moment and then shook his head. "I'm not really sure."

"He knew you, or about you," Elyssa said, staring at them both expectantly.

"We should start with the covens and cultists," Jenna noted. "Though that could be a long list. Seems like new things sprout up here every Halloween."

"I'll get Angela working on it back at headquarters," Sam said. "I'd like to get into the autopsy. I'll call Jackson, see if Adam Harrison has any sway up here."

"Adam has sway everywhere," Jenna assured him.

Adam Harrison, the dignified philanthropist who'd finally organized his little army of psychic researchers into an FBI unit, did seem to have sway everywhere. He was a good man, one who'd made a great deal of money and managed to keep his principles. His son, dead in a car accident in high school, had been one of those special people with an unusual ability. Eventually, Adam had learned that his son was not the only one.

"Excuse me," Sam told them. "I'm going to make some calls. You know Devin Lyle and Craig Rockwell are from this area, too. We might need some help covering the ground."

"Good idea," Jenna said. In all the rush she'd forgotten that her co-agents were also from Salem. Then again, Elyssa's hysterical call that morning had made her forget everything. "Hopefully, they're not already on assignment."

"We'll see," Sam said, and headed out to the living room where he could call privately.

Uncle Jamie glanced at his watch. "Susan is due back soon. What are we going to say to her? I can't encourage a child to lie to her parents, but Susan and Matt will see her locked away in an institution."

"I'm not a child," Elyssa reminded them. "Come June, I'll be both a high school grad and over eighteen."

"And that means you'll stop loving and caring for your parents?" Jamie asked.

"Of course not. But Uncle Jamie, they think I'm crazy."

"It's going to be fine," Jenna said. "Your mom knows that you called me, right?"

Elyssa nodded. "I seem to have the gift. My mom doesn't, so she'll never understand."

"Some people never do," Jenna said. "But that doesn't mean she doesn't love you. So what we're going to do is this. You'll say you can't help but be concerned and worried. And I'll say that Sam and I have come because we've realized just how long it's been since we've been back here, so why not check out this situation for you. How's that?"

She looked at Jamie and Elyssa.

"Omission in itself can be a lie," her uncle said. "But, okay, it's not a lie."

The admission came just in time, as the doorbell rang. They could hear the door open and Sam's deep voice as he introduced himself to Susan and Matt Adair, Elyssa's parents.

"Jenna," Susan Adair said, hurrying across the room with a huge hug. "Have you had a chance to speak with Elyssa? You've explained that, while it's sad and tragic, poor Mr. Bradbury took his own life. All I think about are his children. This will be so hard for them."

"Not to worry," Jenna said. "We've assured Elyssa that we'll look into it all and that she needs to worry about school and midterms."

Sam laid his hands on Jenna's shoulders. "It never hurts to be thorough. That's what the bureau is all about. But Jenna is right. Elyssa doesn't have to worry or be concerned about a thing."

"See," Susan said, turning to her daughter triumphantly. "That's all good."

Matt Adair had been hovering by the door, watching the reunion. He was fit—an athletic man, coaching football at the local high school. They were quite the odd couple. Susan, Irish-looking with carrot red hair and amber eyes, a ball of fire and energy. Matt, except for when he was on the football field, a model of quiet and calm.

He greeted Jenna with a hug, then said, "I never like to say there's nothing to worry about."

Elyssa let out a sigh. "He's worried because I was babbling, and he's afraid my peers are going to make fun of me. That's the least of my worries. Honestly, Dad. My feet are on the ground, and I've never been swayed by peer pressure."

And, to the best of Jenna's knowledge, she hadn't been. Elyssa was bright and happy. She made friends because she was honestly interested in others and enjoyed meeting people. Between them, Susan and Matt had raised her right. A daughter open to new experiences, but comfortable in her own.

"It's always smart to be cautious," Uncle Jamie murmured. "Now, how about some food. I've taken the liberty of ordering out. Italian. And I think the delivery person just drove up."

"I'll head out and get it," Sam offered.

"And I'll give you a hand," Matt said.

"Wait," Susan said. "Why does anyone need to be cautious? This was a suicide. Right? Our daughter found the poor man and that's that."

But no one answered her.

Jenna hurried to help Uncle Jamie with plates and Elyssa found silverware and glasses. The delivery order included lasagna, salad, and breadsticks and the next few minutes were spent passing food around.

"What's new in town?" Sam asked, when everyone was satisfied with a plate filled to their liking.

"They keep building ugly new structures," Matt said.

"It used to be so quaint here. But commercialism is ruining the place," Susan added, shaking her head.

"But a lot of the old shops are still around, right?"

"Oh, yes, and more." Susan said. "New England seems to be moving into an age of diversity. We now have a large Asian population."

"And Hispanic," Matt said.

"Russian, too. Mostly Eastern Europeans," Uncle Jamie said. "We have a new family from Estonia at my church these days, and a number of Polish."

Susan shrugged and smiled. "And islanders. South Americans and Southerners."

Jenna had to laugh. The way Susan spoke, it seemed that Southerners were the most foreign of anyone who'd moved to Salem. "The world moves all over these days. People go different places for work, to study, and some just to live."

"I actually love all of the different languages, the people and accents," Susan said. "But I have to say, if this weren't my home, I don't know if I would have moved here."

Jenna was curious. "Why?"

"Snow," Elyssa said. "Mom hates the snow."

"I don't hate the snow. I hate shoveling snow. And chipping the windows covered with ice."

"Oh, mom, you love Salem. We couldn't pry you out of here with a fire poker."

Elyssa seemed exceptionally happy. As if what had been so horrible was not half so bad anymore.

"Tell me about the new shops in town," Jenna said, glancing at Sam. No better way to learn the lay of the land than ask the locals.

"There's a great place called Down River on Essex Street," Matt said. "I love it. All kinds of books, new and used, and wonderful art and artifacts."

"It's owned by one of the silly Southerners who moved north to shovel snow," Susan said. "Pass the garlic bread, will you please?"

"And there's a restaurant and shop that opened near there," Matt told them. "Indian, from across the ocean. Great food. Beautiful saris and shirts."

"Too much curry, that's the way I see the food," Susan said.

"What about the old places?"

"Most of them are still around. And, of course, there are a number of covens. I think we also have people practicing Santeria or voodoo or something like that." Susan shook her head. "Evil spells." And her hand with the fork shivered halfway to her mouth.

"Most people," Uncle Jamie said, "whether they're practicing Santeria or voodoo or if they're Baptists or Catholics or Episcopalians, are good people. Today's Wiccans tend to be lovely, not wanting to hurt anyone."

"You really do see the good in everyone," Susan said.

"Most religions are good. What men and women do with that sometimes is the problem. I just don't go assuming they're out to do evil."

"I hope not," Matt said. "Halloween seems to bring out all of the kooks. Especially in Salem. And we did have that terrible incident with those murders just a year or two back."

"We know about that," Sam said. "We had colleagues involved with the investigation."

"We're going to hope that everyone behaves for Halloween," Susan said sternly. "And plan on all good things, right, Elyssa?"

The young girl nodded. "I'm going to the school dance, then a party at Nate's house. I'm going to be an angel. Not costume-wise. I'm going as Poison Ivy. But I'll be an angel."

When it was time for the Adair family to leave, Elyssa caught Jenna by the door and gave her a tight hug once again. "Thank you so much for coming. You've made me feel sane again."

Jenna smiled and watched the family go.

As the car drove down the street, Sam turned to Uncle Jamie. "Okay, so what's really going on around here?"

Jamie stared at him. "What do you mean?"

"I know you're in on everything happening. Santeria, voodoo. What else is there that we need to know about?"

The older man sighed and shrugged. "We do have two voodoo priestesses in town. They read tarot cards and do palm reading. But that's not new for Salem, as you know. A few neighbors have complained about chickens. I assume they're being used in their services."

"And the Wiccans? Have you heard of anything troubling there?"

"They're like any group, squabbling now and then."

"Were any of the groups upset about the things going on at the mortuary?" Sam asked.

"Now that I think of it, there was a town meeting. Quite honestly, it was all the usual. A woman complaining that having the mortuary be a theme park attraction for Halloween made fun of witchcraft. She objected to the image of everyone who practiced the Wiccan religion being portrayed as a broom-riding, warty old woman. Someone else was complaining that the haunted house took away from the historic value of the town. Another guy gave a great oratory about the freedom of being in America. Be Wiccan, a Buddhist, whatever, and accept all else. Some clapped for him, some said freedom came with responsibility and respect. But cooler heads prevailed. It's Halloween and every self-respecting town has to have a great haunted attraction. Besides, Salem makes a lot of money at Halloween."

"Think you can make us a list of names of people who seemed to be heading toward the fanatical stage on their speeches?" Sam asked.

"Absolutely."

"You talked to Jackson?" Jenna asked Sam.

He nodded. "Devin Lyle and Craig Rockwell are going to come straight here from a situation in San Diego. They'll be here by tomorrow night, or the next morning at the latest."

"That's Halloween," Jenna said.

"I'm off," Sam said, smiling at the other two. "Care to join me?"

"And where are you going, and what do you think you can discover at this time of night?" Uncle Jamie asked.

"Angela and the home office are online, seeing what they can find out. Thankfully, everyone has a blog or is on Facebook these days. They like to bitch, so we may find something out through their posts. So where else does one get the skinny on what's happening? The best local bar in the center of the action. Except, what would that be now? Hard to say. So I'll just hop from one bar to another and see what's there."

Chapter 3

"There," Jenna said, motioning with her head.

"Where, what?" Sam asked.

They'd entered a relatively new place on Essex Street called The Sorcerer's Brew. Nicely adorned with lots of carved wood and old kegs and trunks for tables and seats. The menu was full of old standards like clam chowder, scrod, fish, meat and chicken, many done up blackened, with cilantro or sriracha sauce. The signature cocktail was also called The Sorcerer's Brew, and they had taps for twenty different beers on draft.

Definitely a tourist stop.

The Peabody Essex museum was just down the street along with a number of the historic houses open to the public. Ghost tours left from the front of nearby shops and a number of store windows offered haunted mazes, 3-D haunted experiences, and slightly twisted versions of the ghosts of Salem, all which utilized various scenes of the condemned coming back to life to curse those who'd accused them. Like most new places that sprang up, the locals checked in now and then. Especially at Halloween, when they were working late and craved a quick bite, a drink, or a cup of tea after work.

Sam followed Jenna's pointed finger and saw a pair of young women seated in a carved wooden booth toward the windows at the front of the restaurant. He followed her as she moved through the crowd.

"Who are they?" he asked.

"Old friends," she told him, and then she grinned. "Actually, you know them. You chaperoned all of us one day years ago."

And he remembered. Part of the teenage wild gang.

"Stephanie," Jenna said. "Audra."

The two women turned, then both sprang to their feet. There was a lot of gushing and hugs. Sam stood by and waited, then he was introduced. Stephanie had long dark hair and was dressed in black jeans and a black sweater. Audra too had long hair, dressed in a black-tailored shirt and long skirt. Stephanie still looked like a girl with big brown eyes and a gamine-like face. Audra cast a more sophisticated appearance.

"My God," Stephanie said, giving him a hug. "I'd heard you two were together now. I didn't get to see either of you when you were here on that awful Lexington House case. But, oh, a big-time lawyer, eh? Do you remember us? Audra and I were the other kids you had to watch that day. We tormented you, didn't we? But we all had these massive crushes on you. It's great to see you. Are you moving back?"

"Of course, I remember both of you," Sam said, lying. Actually, he didn't remember either of them, only Jenna. "It's great to see you. And no, we're not moving back. We're just here to visit."

"Sit down, join us, can you?" Audra asked.

Sam took a seat on the wooden bench next to Stephanie. Jenna slid beside Audra.

"We know why you're here," Audra said.

"We do?" Stephanie said. "I actually don't. What's going on?"

Audra drew an elegantly polished purple nail along the sweat on her beer mug. "The death at the mortuary. Elyssa Adair found the body."

"That's true," Sam said.

Jenna looked at him, shrugged, and went with his direction. "She was upset and called me. So that's why we're here."

"The whole thing is a little strange, isn't it?" Sam said.

Audra agreed with a shrug. "If that's what I did for a living, manage haunted houses, and I decided to do it all in, I would think that doing something like that would be a great final statement to the world."

Stephanie gasped. "You don't think he committed suicide, do you?"

"We don't really know anything at all," Sam said. "We're just here with the family."

"Did you two get married?" Stephanie asked.

"Not yet," Sam said. "But it's coming. What do you two know about the mortuary and the haunted house? Anything odd going on there?"

"You mean besides a man found hanged to death?" Audra asked.

"Yeah. Besides that."

Stephanie shrugged and said, "The paranormal people aren't happy about renting to the haunted house people. They're above all that, you know. And the haunted house people just think that the paranormal people are crazy. Micah is kind of a self-important jerk and Jeannette Mackey thinks that she's a serious psychic and that all the Wiccan palm and tarot readers in town are idiots. But when it comes to keeping the mortuary going, they force themselves to get along. Oh, my God. You don't think Micah murdered him, do you?"

"We don't know what to think," Sam said.

"But you've come home to solve this murder, haven't you?" Stephanie asked. "This is your home, Sam, right?"

He nodded. "Absolutely."

Jenna looked at Audra. "Are you in a coven?"

"I practice Wicca, but no, I'm not in a coven. I like practicing the tenets on my own. A lot of people don't really practice, they just join covens and then charge for tarot and palm readings and whatever else. Then they charge to be mentors. I don't like the charging part of it, so I practice on my own."

"Oh, come on, there are good covens in the area," Stephanie said.

"Some," Audra agreed. "But only a few."

"So do Wiccans argue with each other?" Sam asked.

"The only argument I know about is between Gloria Day and Tandy Whitehall," Audra said. "Old school versus new school, and all about money. Gloria runs the Silver Moon Festival throughout October. Tandy is much younger and has started doing some really wickedly wild parties. They're always vying for the most publicity. Everyone else is divided. Some support the new, others the old. But mainly they just bitch about each other privately."

"Then there's that idiot who went to court to support the drunk who killed a guy in the crosswalk. Said he was a warlock and that he was going to hex everyone," Stephanie said.

"Male witches aren't warlocks. They're witches, right?" Sam said, frowning.

"They are," Audra agreed, flicking a hand in the air. "At least, in my circles they are. But there are zillions of diverse ways to be a Wiccan or practice the Old Religion. There's Shamanic, Celtic, Gardnerian, and more, not to mention paganism, Pantheists, and Druids. What we all have in common is a love and respect for nature. Most of the holidays are about the same, speaking of which, Halloween is Samhain to us.

"Anything else going on?" Sam asked.

"I need another beer if we're going to play twenty questions," Stephanie said. "And you two haven't had anything to drink yet. What's happened to the service around here?"

"I'll take care of it," Sam said. "I guess they're swamped. What are you all drinking?"

"Local brew. Black Witches Ale. Give it a try," Stephanie said.

"Okay, four mugs of Black Witches Ale coming up."

Sam walked over to the bar and waited his turn, observing those who were there, some in street clothes, others in partial costume. Those were the ones who worked at the historical or Halloween venues, glad to be out of Puritan or creature garb for the night.

"Every place in Salem," an older man next to him said, and sighed. He shook his head, then glanced at Sam apologetically, as if realizing he'd spoken aloud. "Sorry—commercialism! Good for Salem, hard on those who live here!"

"It is almost Halloween," Sam said.

"Can't wait until it's over."

Sam offered his hand and introduced himself. "I'm from here; home for a visit with some family of a friend."

They shook hands.

"The place has changed. I remember when Laurie Cabot started up with the first witch shop. You would have been young."

"I remember," Sam said.

"Nowadays, we got everything. This morning, damn if there wasn't a chicken head out on the embankment by my place."

Sam asked him where he lived, which was just a few blocks down from where they were, not far from the Elizabeth Montgomery *Bewitched* statue.

"We have Creole neighbors. Don't know what they're practicing, but come on, chicken heads?" The man sighed again. "My wife does say that Mrs. DuPont makes a heck of a chicken pot pie, though. Chicken heads and suicides. I'm telling you, the real stuff going on here now is worse than Halloween. Good for the economy, but crazy for regular folks."

"You're referring to John Bradbury's death?" Sam asked.

"I am. Sad thing. Nice guy. He'd come in here now and then. I'm a realtor and have some late nights. Anyway, Bradbury was always excited about bringing his artistic craft home to Salem. That's what he called it.

He loved the old mortuary up there. He told me he wished he could buy it and, if ever he could, he'd turn it into a permanent attraction. Put more history in it, that kind of a thing. He loved the history of Halloween and how the Christian church managed to combine with the pagan ways."

The harried bartender came to them and Sam let the older man place his order first, then asked for the beers. The man thanked him and told Sam he'd be seeing him and moved on. As Sam collected the four steins of Black Witches Ale, he heard a couple at the bar arguing.

"Don't do it," the man warned.

"She's a bitch, and I'm going to take her down," the woman said defiantly.

"You're being ridiculous. There are enough people here to make everyone successful and happy. And, besides, that has nothing to do with practicing what we believe."

"It has to do with pride and with that nasty little bitch Gloria Day trying to take over from everyone else."

"Stop talking," the man said. "Someone will hear you."

"Maybe someone out there is practicing black magic. Not a Wiccan religion, but pure Satanism. Bradbury talked against her, and look where he is."

"It was a suicide," the man said.

"Maybe. Maybe not."

Sam pretended to get thrown against the man's arm. When the fellow turned to look at him, he quickly apologized. "Sorry. It's so busy in here."

"It's okay," the man said.

"I don't remember it being this crazy. I'm from here, but...wow. Sam Hall, by the way. Nice to meet you, since I nearly sloshed beer on you."

The man frowned. "Sam Hall. You're that big-time attorney. Sorry, I'm David Cromwell and this is my wife, Lydia."

"Nice to meet you both," Sam said and decided not to tell them that he wasn't really practicing law anymore. "By the way, what should I do on Halloween? I hear there are all kinds of things going on and since I haven't been home in ages, I wouldn't mind some advice."

"Tandy Whitehall's Moonlight Madness," Lydia said. "Tandy has been here forever and she's the real deal. She gets fabulous bands and, if you get a reading at the party, it'll be a good one. It's just lovely."

David Cromwell had lowered his head and was gritting his teeth. Bingo. Sam knew that he had hit the core of their argument. Lydia was a huge Tandy Whitehall fan. In the morning, he'd find out how vicious and divisive that fight might be. John Bradbury was dead, and he'd apparently been vocal against the usurper as well.

"Thanks so much," Sam said.

He headed back to the table with the beers. Stephanie and Audra were bringing Jenna up to date on what was going on with their families. They all paused to thank him as he returned.

"Slow waiter," Jenna teased, looking at him.

He sensed she was ready to go, as he'd caught her glance at him while he talked to the Cromwells at the bar. A few minutes later, Jenna yawned and said that they needed to get some sleep.

"And who knows? Uncle Jamie might still have a curfew going for me."

Audra said, "If you think we can help you in any way, please, don't hesitate to let us know."

"Thanks," Sam said.

"Don't look now," Audra said, "but that's Jeannette Mackey. See the athletic looking woman who just went up to the bar? She's Micah Aldridge's VP or whatever for the paranormal part of the mortuary."

"Really?" Sam muttered.

"I know her," Audra said. "She's older than we are by several years, but I know I've met her a few times. She was on the news a lot, even in Boston. Interviewed on her views on the past and the present and parapsychology."

"I remember when she first started talking about creating a 'true home for the power of the mind,'" Sam said.

He saw the bartender greet her and hand her a large glass of whiskey. "We should pay our respects on the way out."

"Definitely," Jenna said.

They bid her friends goodnight. Sam slipped an arm around Jenna and together they headed for the attractive woman swilling down the drink that had been poured for her.

"Miss Mackey," Sam said.

The woman spun around and stared at Sam, a little wild-eyed, then said, "Samuel Hall, attorney, right?"

"Correct. And this is Jenna Duffy. I believe you two have met somewhere along the line, too."

"Jenna, yes, how are you? You and Elyssa are cousins, right?"

"You have a good memory. We came up to support the family. I understand you and John Bradbury worked together. We just stopped by to say how sorry we are."

"Thank you. I had tremendous respect for John. It was an incredibly important job he had. His company was growing bigger and bigger and his ideas and management were brilliant. I can't tell you how much money the haunted house aspect makes, and what wonderful funds we received because of it. Survival, really. Oh, not that I like a haunted house. But, hey, it was so important I'd play a part in all the schlock when necessary." She looked at the empty glass in her hand. "We're all in shock. Of course, Micah is taking it in stride. I guess he is the stronger one, between us."

"If there's anything we can do, please let us know," Jenna said.

"Of course. And if you need me for anything." Her voice trailed. "A suicide. John. I still can't believe it."

"Actually, we're not sure we do believe it," Sam said.

"What?" Jeannette asked, sounding stunned.

"We'll be looking into it," Jenna assured her.

"Of course, you will, of course. As sad as it is, oh, my God. You think that someone would have harmed him?" Jeannette asked.

"Do you know of any enemies he might have had?" Jenna asked.

"John? None. He was polite and courteous to everyone. He had a bit of a problem with Gloria Day, but that's a long story. Even so, he was still decent to her. She just didn't like playing off Tandy Whitehall's thunder." She lowered her voice. "And the Wiccans, you never know what they're up to." She let out a soft sigh. "Excuse me, will you? I'm going to go home and try to get some sleep."

"Us, too," Sam said. "I just want you to know that we're sorry."

She thanked them, turned, and hurried out.

"What do you think?" Sam asked Jenna.

"I think we have a lot to look into."

The streets were still crazed with activity. It was nearing midnight and there were parties galore around town. Children and adults alike seemed to enjoy dressing up for the season. They turned the corner to cut down by Burying Point and the memorial to those who'd been condemned to hang along with Giles Corey, "pressed" to death. They passed a few late night ghost tours, the guides dressed in Puritan garb.

Many people believed Salem to be one of the most haunted cities in the world. Easy to understand why. There were those who'd been condemned to death, along with those who died imprisoned, or others who went mad from fear or from what was done to them. A rich history permeated, one that needed to be remembered. Fear could cause normally decent people to do terrible things. Or, even worse, to practice the sin of silence, too afraid to speak out against injustice.

Jenna stopped by the memorial with its stone benches, each dedicated to one of the victims.

"John Proctor spoke out, and he died for it," she said. "I always think about that. He threatened Mercy Warren, his servant girl, with a beating if she didn't stop with the fits, and it worked once."

"You believe all of this has something to do with the witchcraft trials and the modern Wiccans?" Sam asked.

She shrugged. "The case that Devin and Rocky worked up here had to do with someone who'd been murdered before she could be tried. And, according to Elyssa, John Bradbury's ghost mentioned something about witches."

"I actually heard a woman back in the bar mention to her husband that John Bradbury had supported Tandy Whitehall against Gloria Day."

"May mean nothing."

"But could be everything. Another guy told me about finding chicken heads by his house. His neighbors, the DuPont family, practice Santeria or a religion that considers chickens to make good sacrificial offerings."

"Maybe they just like fresh meat at dinner?"

"At least we've got the feel for Halloween in Salem," he told her, slipping an arm around her shoulders as they continued to walk. "I want in on the autopsy. It'll take place tomorrow. Adam Harrison is going to work with the governor, who will call the mayor. I also want to get to the Mayberry Mortuary. It was closed once the body was found. The police and forensic people probably haven't finished with it just yet."

"If they suspect just a suicide," Jenna murmured.

"I don't know what they suspect. The lead detective on the case is a guy named Gary Martin. I don't know the man. I hope it's someone Devin or Rocky might know."

Jenna shook her head. "I don't know the name either."

"I should be able to meet with Martin in the morning and get into the autopsy."

"I'll head to the Mayberry Mortuary," Jenna said.

They came to the cemetery and Sam stopped. He could see the old tombstones with their death's heads, cherubs, angels, and other decorations, opaque and haunting in the moonlight. The main gates were locked at this time of night and it was, of course, illegal for anyone to enter. He thought for a moment he saw movement by one of the gnarled old trees.

"What is it?" Jenna asked.

He shook his head. "Nothing. Let's get back and get some sleep. It's been a long day."

She agreed.

The crowds had thinned, a few groups here and there, less as they left the cemetery and some of the major attractions behind and headed down the street that led to Uncle Jamie's house.

As they turned a corner, Jenna said, "There's another one, or the same guy on a costume bender. Another boo-hag."

She was right. Across the street, a group in costume was walking toward the wharf, heading back to one of the new hotels near the water. And there was someone in the same costume that had jumped onto their car.

A boo-hag.

Sam had been born and raised in Salem and he'd never even heard of a boo-hag before. Now he'd seen two in as many days.

The group was walking with their backs toward Sam and Jenna. Suddenly, the man in the boo-hag costume turned, stared their way for a moment, then headed off.

"That was eerie," Jenna said. "Movie monsters and most creatures seem almost ho-hum around here, but that costume gets to you."

"A boo-hag," Sam said. "Definitely creepy."

He didn't mention that there was something more. The way the eyes seemed to focus on them, the way they seemed to burn, even at a distance, as if they were formed of fiery red-gold, burning like the flames of hell.

Chapter 4

Sam knew that they often dealt with terrible things. That was the occupation he and Jenna had both chosen. Partly because of their "gifts," and partly because they wanted to make a difference. But this situation seemed more personal. He'd intended to give Jenna all the space she needed. But alone, in the darkness of their room at Uncle Jamie's, she turned to him with a sweet and urgent passion. The warmth of her naked body next to his, flesh against flesh, and the fever that seemed to burn in her became electric. No words, just her moving against him, touching, a feather-light caress at first, then a passionate love, both tender and urgent. He held her afterward, naked and slaked against him, and he thought that they both would sleep well.

Home was wonderful.

But home was also a place where nightmares could be rekindled.

He didn't want her facing any demons in her mind. But that night Sam was the one to dream. He saw something coming toward them out of a strange and misty darkness. Red, with shimmering golden eyes that seemed to burn with evil.

Then he realized that the thing wasn't coming at him.

He wasn't next to Jenna anymore. She was some distance away, sleeping, laid out on the bed, eyes closed, a half smile on her face.

And the thing was going for her.

He tried to run, to block the horrible menace from reaching the woman he loved. No matter how hard he tried, he was slowed down by the thick red mist.

The thing was now on Jenna, leaning over her, stiffening, inhaling, as if prepared to suck the life from her. The red mist became thicker and thicker. He realized he was fighting, straining, trying so hard to reach her. But it was no longer red mist that held him back. Instead, the barrier had become a sea of blood.

He woke with a start.

Morning.

His phone ringing.

An aura of fear stayed with him and he fought it; reaching for the phone and checking on Jenna, who was just beginning to rouse.

Jackson was calling. The right people had talked to the right people, and the FBI had been officially asked into the investigation. While suicide in the death of John Bradbury was a valid theory, the media had gone wild over the whole situation. Whispers of foul play ran rampant. He thanked Jackson for the assist and hung up.

"That's perfect," Jenna said, when he explained the call.

"I have to get to the autopsy," he told her.

"And I'll head to the mortuary."

"Maybe you should come with me," he said, recalling some of the dream.

"Don't be silly. We need to move fast on this. There are so many people we're going to have to interview, so much we have to find out. We have to divide the load. I know the mortuary, but we need to know the layout, how someone might have gotten in. That can only come from a visit."

She was right and he knew it.

He still didn't want to be away from her.

"Devin and Rocky will be here—"

"We can't wait on them," she said, frowning then smiling. "Sam, I'm a good agent. I was an agent before you were an agent, remember? I'll be careful. I promise."

He hesitated. "I had a nightmare," he said.

"You did?"

"A boo-hag was after you."

She smiled. "Sam, boo-hags aren't real."

"The one in the street was real. So we have to watch out."

"I swear, I'll be careful."

"Maybe—"

"Sam, I'm good at what I do. And when you're back from the autopsy, we'll meet up and go together from there."

He rose.

She was already up, heading to the shower. He started to follow her. She laughed, paused, and told him, "No time for that. I'll be right out. We need to move this morning."

"So you think you're that irresistible?" he asked her.

She grinned. "In a shower, you're irresistible."

And she closed the door on him.

"Nice lip service," he told her through the door.

"Lip service is later," she said.

He grinned at that, stared at the closed door for a minute, and then gathered his clothing for the day. He couldn't be unreasonable. He'd had a nightmare. Part of coming home, perhaps. And yet, in their world, nightmares could be real or, at a minimum, whispers of threats to come.

* * * *

"Hauntings and Hallucinations rents the space from us for the event," Micah Aldridge told Jenna.

It was just nine in the morning but she'd arrived at the Mayberry Mortuary to meet with Micah. Sam had headed for the autopsy and his meeting with Gary Martin. Adam Harrison had performed his usual magic. The FBI wasn't taking *lead* on the investigation—the situation didn't warrant it yet—but they were to be given access to information and leave to investigate. She hadn't met Martin and hoped that he didn't intend to dismiss the death as a suicide with no possibility of foul play. Things were always easier when everyone cooperated with everyone else. Most of the time it worked that way. But every once in a while they hit a local law enforcement officer who was more proprietorial, not wanting federal interference.

"I have to admit," Micah said. "I kind of loathed the idea of having something so schlocky here when we are trying to do real research. But bills have to be paid and we make enough from the Halloween rental to carry us through the year."

She nodded. "Makes sense."

She studied the beautiful old building. By daylight, the skeletons, spiders webs, and jack-o-lanterns all appeared to be just nicely arranged paper and props, nothing more. By night, with special lighting, the place appeared eerie, especially the cemetery surrounding it. When it wasn't

Halloween season, the place still cast a certain melancholy about it, a poignancy that perhaps reflected the shadows of lives gone by.

"You've been here before, haven't you?" Micah asked.

"I took an historic tour when I was about fifteen," Jenna said. "It's been a while. But I would like to take a look inside."

They entered through the foyer. Double doors led into a massive living room and to the ornate stairway that led up to the second floor. The living room was filled with creatures, spider webs, a giant tarantula, and other oddities. On one wall a painting had flesh when first looked at, but turned skeletal from a different angle. A grand piano, complete with a skeleton player, sat by the windows to the porch. By night, the interior lights would show him in an eerie symphony.

"They do a good job," Jenna said. "Where are the stairs down to the basement?"

"John made it all possible," a female voice said.

She turned to see a young woman entering from the foyer. Attractive, with a wealth of long dark hair and a pretty face, but her eyes welled with tears as she approached.

"I'm Naomi Hardy."

"Jenna Duffy."

"Naomi and John Bradbury worked hand in hand," Micah said. "His death has been hard on her."

Concern filled Micah's voice.

"John was a true visionary," Naomi said. "He went to shows across the country, always looking for the newest innovations in creepy, chilling, *fun* scares. But he insisted we keep some real history too, to go along with all the whacko legend and scary movie stuff. He was so good. Head of the artistic branch, and every year at Halloween, he managed this place himself. I still can't believe he's gone."

"I am truly sorry for your loss," she said.

"Jenna is with the FBI."

"You're here over a suicide?"

"Elyssa Adair, who found the body, is my cousin," Jenna said. "I'm really here to help her through this."

The explanation seemed to satisfy Naomi.

"John had the best job in the world. But then he'd had such a horrible divorce. His wife should have been shot. He'd had some drug problems as a kid and she dragged every bit of that into court, destroying his reputation. He had a hard time getting over it. All his success, and he could barely see his own children."

Which made the ex a definite suspect.

"Is the wife still around?" Jenna asked.

"No. That was the first thing the police asked. But she was nowhere near here. Home with the kids and she hadn't seen John since their last court date, months ago. She went on TV. Blamed his past, his drug problems, everything on him."

Tears welled in Naomi's eyes, which she brushed aside before asking, "What are you doing here at the mortuary?"

"Tying up the loose ends."

Naomi shrugged, as if uninterested. "If you'll excuse me, we're reopening tonight and now it's all on me. Micah, I'll be down at the ticket booth if you need me. Jenna, a pleasure to meet you, even under these circumstances."

She and Micah walked upstairs. Without darkness and actors, all of the haunting paraphernalia seemed worn and sad. Micah pointed out what was usually the tarot card reading and séance room. Another bedroom was used for psychic testing. She was interested in the entire layout, but really wanted to get to the basement to see if she could sense or feel anything. Elyssa wasn't lying. John Bradbury had appeared to her. But it would be helpful if that ghost would speak with her or Sam.

"Is there only one entrance to the basement?" she asked.

Micah nodded. "From the house, yes. The stairs are in the back of the kitchen. There's also an entrance from the back driveway that slopes down to a door. I guess it made for easy deliveries when the place was used as a funeral home."

Micah seemed fine about going down to the basement, but then again, he'd been alone here when she arrived. If the place was haunted in any way, Micah certainly didn't care.

She followed him to the ground floor landing and around the grand staircase to a door and more stairs that led down.

"It's a mess," Micah told her. "The police moved just about everything. Naomi will be taking over as manager and she'll see to it that everything is in order before tonight."

"Reopening already?" Jenna asked.

He shrugged. "I'm truly sorry. I liked John. He was a great guy. But life goes on and we have to pay the bills."

"Yes, I guess so," she murmured.

"The stairs are fairly narrow," Micah said. "In the old days, the dead came in through the back entry, and the coffins went back out that same way. Hauntings and Hallucinations carries some major liability insurance and we have strict rules about how many people can come through at one time. We're not the responsible party here, just the lessor, but we don't want anything bad to happen to anyone. Well, dead is bad, but the poor guy did himself in. You know, I saw John every day for the last couple of months and I had no idea he was so depressed."

Jenna didn't reply or correct him. Better to stay silent.

They'd reached the basement. The long stone embalming tables remained, each piled high with Halloween decorations. The police had indeed made a mess.

Micah pointed. "In the nooks and cubicle areas we have motion-activated creatures and characters. You can see the giant alien there, the werewolf over here, the vampire and mummy. That crazed killer over there scares the bejesus out of most visitors. Over there is where it happened."

She studied the cubicle, empty except for a giant iron hook that had long been attached to the ceiling above. The rope by which John Bradbury had hung had been removed, but the black lighting set up by the haunted house company remained. She thought that the basement, with its stone foundation pillars, wooden beams, and strewn paraphernalia seemed not eerie, but sad. The soft lighting made if look almost as if surrounded by a red mist. She walked over to where Bradbury had died.

"What were these crevices for?" she asked.

"I really don't know." He paused. "Poor John."

She stood still and wished Micah wasn't with her. Some alone time might be beneficial here.

"The exit from the basement is over this way," Micah said. "We have visitors leave the house via the basement and walk back up the path to the parking lot when they've finished the tour."

He walked toward the back door.

Jenna hovered a moment, waiting, standing still, trying to imagine what had gone on when Bradbury had died.

"Jenna?" Micah called to her.

"Coming," she said.

She waited another few beats, then turned to join him at the exit.

And it hit her.

A movement in the air, a change in the temperature, the sense that they were not alone. She felt a brush against her cheek, and heard a whispered voice in the red mist aura.

I did not die by my own hand.

* * * *

The autopsy happened down in Boston where the Office of the Chief Medical Examiner was located. Sam was pleased to discover that the medical officer on duty was Dr. Laura Foster, a woman he'd worked with several times when he practiced law in Boston. She was bright, determined, and good at her job. There was even a Salem connection. Laura was the descendant of a woman accused of witchcraft during the craze. Her ancestor wasn't hanged. Instead, she died of the horrible conditions in the jail where she was held.

Detective Gary Martin was there too. He was pushing fifty, with short-cropped steel-gray hair. When he'd shaken hands with Sam, Martin had expressed surprise that the FBI had interest in an apparent suicide, but seemed to accept Sam's explanation that they were involved only because of family.

"If there's one thing I've learned," Martin said. "It's that you can never be sure of anything. With John Bradbury, it certainly appears he killed himself."

"It could have been made to look like suicide," Sam said.

Martin appeared skeptical. "Like I say. Anything's possible. Maybe the autopsy will tell us something we don't know."

They stood off to the side while Laura Foster went through the preliminaries, then made a Y incision in the chest and dictated her notes. Death appeared to have come from a broken neck. Otherwise, John Bradbury had been a healthy, forty-five-year-old man, with a strong heart and clear lungs. The last meal remained in the stomach. Clam chowder, white fish, greens. Everything was recorded.

When she stopped speaking, Martin asked, "Suicide?"

"Could be," Laura said. "But, I doubt it."

Sam was listening carefully.

"I'm not a forensics expert," she said, "or a detective. The rope was taken and bagged as evidence yesterday. I saw it. From the way it was tied and the way he hanged, I can't see how he could have slipped it around his own neck. Also, these abrasions here, on the side of the neck. They suggest he was dragged while the rope was in place, choking him." She pointed at the body. "Marks here suggest he was digging at the rope before he died. This man was fighting and kicking. That's what broke his neck. He died fast, much quicker than simple strangulation."

"If he killed himself," Martin said, "he might have been fighting to the end. Perhaps regrets?"

Laura shook her head. "I can't say definitively death was by his own hand."

"So you're calling it a murder?" Martin asked.

Sam remained stoic, practicing something he learned a long time ago as a trial lawyer. Never let them know what you're thinking.

"I can't call this a suicide," Laura said.

"Just great," Martin said.

So much for an open and shut investigation.

"I'm sorry," Laura said. "I'll be doing more testing, but I suggest you start investigating this as a murder."

"Can you give us a time of death?" Sam asked.

"No more than sixteen or seventeen hours. So I'm saying between the hours of two and four, yesterday afternoon."

Martin left the room.

"He didn't want a murder," Laura said to him.

"No one ever does. Thank you for being stubborn."

"I'm not being stubborn, Sam. You know me. I call it the way I see it." She hesitated, nodding to her assistant, who was waiting to sew up the corpse. "It's just science—and justice, right?"

"Absolutely."

He stepped closer to the body. Sometimes, though not often, the dead could be reached by simple touch. But John Bradbury's spirit was not with them in the room.

He thanked Laura again.

"I hate it when people use Salem," she said. "When they do something like this, stringing a man up as if he was one of the victims from the old witch craze. It's mocking at its worst. Ignore Mr. I-Want-A-Suicide out there and catch this killer."

"Martin's not a bad guy. He was just going with what appeared to be obvious. The word was out that John Bradbury had been having a bad time lately. An excellent candidate for suicide. But we owe it to him to find the truth."

She nodded. "Glad you're on this, Sam."

He left the room. Martin had already stripped off the paper mask he'd worn inside. Sam did the same.

"Who the hell murders a guy like that?" Martin asked. "And how did you know?"

"I didn't," Sam said. "We're involved only because of Jenna's cousin, Elyssa."

Martin shook his head. "I guess that's your story and you're sticking to it. You Feds gripe my tail. You just come and go as you please, sticking your noses into what should be a local matter."

Sam tried to be diplomatic. He'd dealt with this attitude before. "We help local authorities solve a crime. That is all our jobs, right?"

"Yeah, I guess it is. You do know that I didn't want this to be murder. It's Halloween season. Patrol cops are going to have their hands full with corralling a ton of costumed drunks. Now there's a murderer running loose among them."

Sam pictured the boo-hag again from last night.

But no boo-hag had sucked the life out of John Bradbury.

No.

That poor man had been murdered.

Chapter 5

"During the afternoon, the only people here would have been me, Jeannette Mackey, John Bradbury, or Naomi Hardy," Micah told Jenna. "There are deliveries during the day. And when we're not open, the doors are supposed to be locked. Of course, we're open during the day in the afternoons for tours, but only if we have tours. They're by appointment only during October. That's not to say that someone might not have left a door or window open."

"No security cameras or alarm system?" Jenna asked.

"Yes, there's an alarm."

Whoever killed John Bradbury had done so in the afternoon before six o'clock since, by then, the actors and guides had reported and there were people coming and going from the basement. She asked Micah about who might have been at the mortuary that afternoon.

"It should have been locked. The only people there were the usual day workers. That's myself and Jeannette Mackey. During the season, it included John Bradbury and Naomi Hardy. I'm not sure when I first saw Naomi that day, but Jeannette and I both came in around eleven. I didn't see or hear anything. John had talked about taking a day off, so we assumed that he had. To be honest, while we like to be the "real" psychic deal and distance ourselves from Halloween hokum, it's all a little bit fun. So we like being a part of it. Participating. Watching." His voice drifted off. "We went through all of this with the police that night. They were dumbfounded that so many people who worked here, and then so many attendees went through, before anyone realized that our swinging corpse was real. There was always a corpse there and things are supposed to look authentic."

"And the police have said that you can reopen tonight?" Jenna asked.

He shrugged. "It seems part of the attraction now. You can rent the room in Fall River where Lizzie Borden hacked her stepmother to death. You can rent the room at the Hardrock Hotel in Florida where Anna Nicole Smith died. And someone died, at some time, in a good percentage of the homes in New England."

"I think it was more than two nights after before you could rent either room," she said. "So the people who should have been here during the day were you, John, Jeannette, and Naomi. And there is a security system. So if someone broke in, you should have known it?"

He shrugged a little unhappily. "Probably. But Jeannette and I were getting ready for a meeting of the Salem Psychic Research Society. We did find a college kid walking around, just looking, not doing anything bad."

"But with this hugely popular attraction going on, you have no cameras, no eyes on the crowd anywhere?"

"We have plenty of eyes," he said. "Every room has what Hauntings and Hallucinations calls 'security guides.' Someone not in costume, but in a black uniform, carrying a flashlight, there to help out in an emergency."

"And the police have a listing of these people? Did they interview the 'security guide' working last night?"

"Of course. It was William Bishop, and he was a basket case. The guides are just simple hires, like the kids who go in costume. Most of them are college aged, a few are retirees. Some are just high school students. We comply fully with all labor laws."

"Micah, I'm not concerned with labor laws. A man is dead."

"It's not my fault he killed himself!"

"But the point is, no one saw him do it."

Micah flushed. "I had no idea John was here. I was upstairs. I have some files beneath the dueling skeletons in the tarot room. Our computers and communications are still up in that room too. Jeannette was with me. Like I said, I don't know what time Naomi got here because I just wasn't paying attention. But she was a little distracted because she hadn't heard from John, and assumed he was taking the night off. I told her not to worry, I'd work the ticket kiosk with her if he didn't come in. She told me they were short a few actors, too. Sally Mansfield, a local housewife who does this every year, was sick with the flu. So Jeannette said she'd be happy to be chopped up or whatever."

"I saw Jeannette last night."

Micah looked at her, surprised. "She said she was going home to bed. She was really upset by what happened. We all cared about John. Poor Naomi. She has to keep this going or the monetary loss will be incredible."

"I've seen businesses closed down for weeks after a tragedy like this. But, I guess you're right, the show must go on."

He hesitated and looked at her suspiciously. "Why are you trying to make a bad situation even more difficult?"

"I'm a special agent with the Federal Bureau of Investigation, Micah. This is my job."

She preferred not to be so pretentious, but sometimes she had to be. And with Micah, it worked.

"Of course, I understand," he said. "But it was a suicide, wasn't it?"

"I don't think so."

"Am I a suspect?"

"Actually, you are," she said pleasantly. "So any assistance you can give me will certainly help in eliminating you."

"Whatever you need. But you know that John's personal life wasn't going well. Oh, my. There was a murderer in here with us? But how? When? I don't see how this can be possible. Oh, my God."

He was panicked, of no help any further. So she decided to leave. "Thanks for your help. I'll call you if I need anything."

She turned to head up the stairs, back to ground level, and out through the front. Micah followed.

"Someone could have come in through the back, through the delivery entrance, I suppose, and we wouldn't have known," he said. "You can't hear. I mean it is a big place."

Outside on the front porch, Jenna noted the quiet location and sad feel to the day. The ticket kiosks seemed cheaply thrown up, the Halloween decorations worn and frayed. Everything was much more magical at night. Naomi Hardy sat at the kiosk, head bowed. Jenna glanced over at the cemetery. Midmorning light was rising, sending streaks of yellow and gold down on the graves. Both the cemetery and house occupied a hill that sloped down to thick forest, the leaves a brilliant collage of orange, crimson, and gold. Past a decaying mausoleum and a weeping angel, she thought she saw something.

A strange flash of darkness and light.

Near the weeping angel and a worn tombstone stood someone in a black cape. Someone with a red face and body. The boo-hag they'd seen the other night. What would someone in costume be doing at the edge of a forlorn graveyard at this time of day, just looking up at the mortuary? She excused herself and headed down the rocky drive toward the cemetery. She leapt over a few tombstones and wove around ancient sarcophagi. But, when she reached the far side and the forest edge, the boo-hag was gone.

She drew her weapon and called out, "FBI. Get the hell out here, whoever you are."

She hadn't really expected a reply, not unless it might come from some holdover partier unsure of where he was from a function the previous night. She moved cautiously into the woods, alert and wary, careful of the leaves and twigs beneath her feet.

And then stopped.

No boo-hag was in sight.

Instead, a woman dangled from a tree limb.

* * * *

"Hanged by the neck until they be dead,'" Detective Gary Martin said, quoting from the death warrants handed down to those executed back in 1692.

Sam watched as a forensic photographer snapped pictures. The victim had been dressed up for display. Their male victim, John Bradbury, had also been decked out in Puritanical garb. Whether this woman often dressed in period clothing for one reason or another, they had no way of knowing. He and Gary Martin had arrived on the scene within minutes of Jenna's call, both on the outskirts of Salem. Once again, Sam was plagued with a feeling of urgency and fear.

The boo-hag.

But Jenna hadn't mentioned a boo-hag. She just said that she'd left the mortuary, come through the graveyard, then walked into the forest, finding a dead woman hanged from a tree. She was calm. No surprise. She was one hell of an agent. She'd touched nothing, securing the scene until forensics and a medical examiner could arrive. They'd asked if Laura Foster might be sent, explaining that they might be looking at a serial killer. He and Martin stood next to Jenna, watching while the crime scene techs did their thing.

"Think this one is a suicide too?" Jenna asked Martin sarcastically.

"Kind of hard to hang yourself from a tree," Martin said. "Unless she climbed up there, then out on the limb, tied the rope, then jumped. Not likely."

Jenna smiled at him. "I'm sorry. I didn't mean to be a pain."

Martin moved around the tree, trying to get a better look at the hanging victim. A large white bonnet hid most of her face and it was difficult—without disturbing the rope—to get a good look at her face.

"It's Gloria Day," Martin said. "She's a big Samhain fest organizer and throws a witches' ball on Halloween. Or it's Samhain, to her, I guess."

"You knew her?" Sam asked.

Martin shook his head. "Not really. I know of her. Her face is on a number of advertisements. This is really going to shake up the community."

Sam and Jenna moved carefully around to where Martin stood to study the corpse too. As they did, the medical examiner's van arrived through the trees. When Laura Foster stepped out, Sam was grateful. They were going to need her on this one. Jenna had not met her, so he introduced the two women and then Laura went to work. Enough photographs had been taken from every angle so the rope was cut and the corpse lowered, laid carefully on a tarp that could be formed into a body bag. A temperature check indicated that the time of death had been somewhere between five and six A.M.

Laura provided as many specifics as she could from a cursory inspection, pointing out the corpse's coloration, the neck had not broken, and she was probably strangled to death, slow and excruciating.

"This is Gloria Day," Laura said.

"Did you know her?" Martin asked.

"I've only seen her. She runs an ad on the local news about her ball every year. She also has a shop and helps promote classes run by some of her coven members. She's kind of a big cheese around here."

"Like John Bradbury?" Jenna asked.

"That's right. But look at the way the rope was tied. It's exactly the same as with Bradbury. When you look at the photographs, you'll see what I mean. I don't believe that either victim tied a rope that way around their own neck." Laura shook her head. "This is going to be one wicked Halloween."

"What about the costume?" Jenna asked.

"She could have worn that herself. She ran the ball, owned a shop, and did some tour guide stuff. I know all that from the ads you can't help but see if you live here. I know she was thirty-eight years old, born in Peoria, Illinois, and a fairly recent transplant to Salem. She arrived in the city in a big way, though her commercial devotion was twitching away."

"Maybe we're looking at a rival coven, or group of covens, or even one of the other sects. Like the voodoo guys, the Haitians, or the Asian-Indians. Maybe I should throw the Catholics and Baptists in there, too," Martin said.

"They're not going to stop," Jenna said.

"Why do you say that?" the detective asked.

She looked up at him. "Someone is trying to recreate the witch craze."

"John Bradbury wasn't a Wiccan," Sam said.

"And neither were any of those executed long ago for signing pacts with the devil," Jenna noted. "People like Bridget Bishop, Rebecca Nurse, Sarah Goode, Susannah Martin—"

"You know their names?" Martin asked.

She nodded. "Elizabeth Howe, Sarah Wilde, George Burroughs, John Willard, Martha Carrier, George Jacobs, Sr., John Proctor, Martha Corey, Mary Eastey, Ann Pudeater, Alice Parker, Mary Parker, Wilmott Redd, Martha Scott, and Samuel Wardell."

"That's impressive," Martin said. "I can add Giles Corey—pressed to death. Had the reputation of being somewhat of a mean son-of-a-bitch, stuck to his guns. He had that famous line, '*More weight!*'" He studied Jenna. "Were you from here? You've got it down."

"Boston. But I spent a lot of time here while growing up. What I'm afraid of is some kind of large-scale plot, or sick deranged thing going on. They're both dressed. No man was hanged first during the real deal. Women got that honor. But there were men condemned and hanged as witches. From what I understand, John Bradbury had a love of local history, but he wasn't a Wiccan. Gloria Day was a big-time Wiccan, apparently famed for her classes and her ball."

Martin looked at Sam. "Let's get a search grid going."

"Sounds good to me."

Martin let out a whistle. A number of uniformed cops hustled over from the road area, around the outskirts of the trees, keeping their distance from the actual murder site until they were given instructions.

"I'm going back to the graveyard," Jenna said. "That's where I came in from."

Sam frowned at her. What had she been doing running around among the tombstones?

"No problem, whatever you need to do," Martin told her.

"I'll join her," Sam said, following Jenna.

To his surprise, Martin came too, leaving his crew to grid search the crime scene.

"You know," Martin said, "it's a 'graveyard' when it's by a church. It's a cemetery when it's freestanding or planned. Most of the plots have names."

Sam was trying to catch up with Jenna, but she was moving ahead quickly.

"Jenna," he called out.

She heard him and stopped.

He reached her. "Did the ghost of John Bradbury find you? What were you doing here? I thought you were searching the house."

She glanced back. Martin stood close to the edge of the forest. "I think he might have whispered to me down in the basement."

"The winged-death's-head is the most popular art on tombstones around here," Martin called, pausing at one of the graves. "The Puritans didn't want anything to do with icons that might suggest Catholicism. 'Life is uncertain, Death is for Sure, Sin is the Wound, and Christ is the Cure,'" he read to them. "Pretty succinct."

"That's a common epitaph in this area," Sam called back.

He looked over at Jenna, waiting for more information.

"It was bizarre," she told him, her green eyes intense. "I followed a costumed figure in there."

"But?"

"I came into the woods and didn't see a soul, except the woman hanged from the tree."

"Cigarette butt," Martin yelled.

"Great. Bag it," Sam called back. "Jenna, what happened to the person you were chasing? You think that they might have done this, or do you think it was a spirit?"

"No, nothing like that. And I don't know if they were a possible suspect or not. The guy in costume might have headed straight for the road, while I cut into the woods deeper. And it's Halloween. Finding someone in costume is going to be ridiculously hard. Half the world around here is going to be dressed up."

"What costume, Jenna?" he asked, holding her shoulders and trying not to grip too hard.

"It was a boo-hag."

Chapter 6

They were sitting in a meeting room at the police station when Craig Rockwell called Sam to say that he and Devin Lyle had landed and were on their way. Sam had seldom been more grateful to have other Krewe members around.

Lt. Bickford P. Huntington, Supervisor for the Criminal Investigations Unit, had called a meeting to inform a task force from Salem and the surrounding areas about the two murders and bring them up to speed on what was known. He had Gary Martin speak and introduced Sam and Jenna as representatives from the federal government. Some there were old friends, some on the force new, not around four years ago when the murders had taken place at Lexington House, which Jenna and Sam had worked.

Sam thought Huntington seemed competent as he laid out all of the information they knew. He also provided a good assessment for what they might be looking for. Someone with a deranged historical sense of revenge, or someone with a contemporary sense of it, or someone who just wanted to kill people. Huntington looked over at Sam and suggested that he provide the group his thoughts. Before he could speak one of the officers spoke up.

"This woman you found today, she was a major commercial-style star Wiccan. Does that mean that we're really looking for someone in a coven?"

The answer was probably yes, but Sam was careful with his reply. He couldn't say that a ghost had told a young woman that his killer had been talking about the witch trials and cults.

"It's my understanding that a feud has been ongoing. So I think it's going to be important to discover if there's someone in some kind of an offshoot cult that might be doing this, not necessarily Wiccan. We all know that today's pagan religions, especially here in Salem, believe in treating everyone with love and respect. Murder would be a terrible sin to anyone truly practicing the Wiccan religion. There are many ways to look at this without stereotyping anyone."

"But, the two victims were killed in the same manner as those executed during the witchcraft trials," another officer said.

"You all know your history here. Anything was witchcraft. If you looked into the future, silly girls playing at love potions, even goodwives trying medicinal herbs, all of that was considered witchcraft. Of course, none of those executed was a witch. It was hysteria, fueled over petty squabbles and simple hatred among the people who lived here then. The pagans, or Wiccans, we have in Salem today have nothing to do with all that. Should we look at strange cults and fundamentalism of any kind, be it Wiccans or another group? Absolutely. Do we need to question people spouting against Gloria Day? Definitely. But the medical examiner's office hasn't even started on the second autopsy yet. Let's see what comes of that."

Jenna was introduced—she smiled and greeted old friends and thanked those she'd worked with before, asking that they be especially vigilant in the areas surrounding the mortuary, graveyard, and forest, and to listen to what they heard around town. "You know Salem. You'll know when something isn't right or when it feels strange. We need to keep a close eye on the mortuary. The first murder apparently happened at a time when those in charge were busy or unaware. And we need to watch out for local situations. Crack pots, cults, culture clashes of any kind."

The meeting ended and Sam and Jenna wound up discussing their next moves in one of the conference rooms while Lieutenant Huntington went on to speak to the press. The community, Sam knew, would be talking about nothing else. But, none of it would stop Halloween or Samhain celebrations. Salem had a life of its own at this time of year. A pulse. A beat. Like a living entity.

Gary Martin was working hard. He hadn't wanted a murder, but he'd wound up with two. His men had retrieved a fair amount of evidence from the forest where Gloria Day's body had been found. All of the cigarette butts, cans, bits and pieces of hair, and everything else would go to the DNA lab. And while TV shows might get their results back in an hour, it would be days, possibly weeks, before these would be ready. Sam harbored no illusions. They were not going to get anything off an old cola can. Their killer wasn't sitting there enjoying a soda before hanging a woman. Results would come from walking and talking and discovering what was going on in the community. Someone had to have seen a car. The hill upon which the mortuary sat alongside the cemetery wasn't in walking distance from town. And Gloria Day's killer had not forced her to walk up the hill then into the forest to be hanged. It made sense that John Bradbury had been in the basement of the mortuary. He worked there. But Gloria Day was another matter. Her shop and school sat in the middle of town, down the street from the Hawthorne Hotel. Had she been lured up there to see something unusual? To participate in some kind of ceremony? Sam was anxious to get to her shop, but he also wanted to know more about the various groups in the community now. And much of it, he thought, needed to be done by himself and Jenna, or Rocky and Devin. The local police were good. But the Krewe team was better.

Alone with Gary Martin and Jenna in the conference room, Sam looked over the files on locals, along with the notes they'd received from Angela Hawkins, Jackson Crow's wife and top assistant. She'd found pages and pages of Facebook, Instagram, Google, and other social media communications that spoke of an all-out verbal war between two factions in the city. Two main rivals were clear. The Coven of the Silver Moon, Gloria Day's group. And the Coven of the Silver Wolf, Tandy Whitehall's people. Each of the two had hives, where the overflow went when there were too many people in a coven. Thirteen was considered the ideal number, but that wasn't etched in stone. Hives, he knew, kept their membership low so as not to become unwieldy, the perfect place for a newly ordained high priest or priestess. Both Day and Whitehall had enjoyed a lot of popularity, their hives numerous and, on occasions like Samhain, they gathered together. In Salem, that usually happened at Gallows Hill, which, frankly, Sam didn't agree with, and for good reason.

Just seemed the wrong place.

"There's been a lot of talk on the web," Martin said, reading through some of the notes Angela had e-mailed. "The word 'bitch' seems overly popular. Gloria Day seems to be accused of being a greedy, manipulative usurper, determined to rule all of Salem. She gives good cause for the world to believe modern-day witches to be old hags with saggy brooms and warts flying across the moon on broomsticks.'" He paused and looked at them. "Now that's just mean. She's old, yes. But certainly not ugly and doesn't have any warts."

Officers had tried to pay a visit to Tandy Whitehall, but she'd not been at her shop, Magical Fantasies, nor at her house. Everyone was on the lookout for her. If she wasn't found soon, sterner measures would be used. Sam believed Whitehall had to know they were looking for her. The media had sniffed out the latest murder with the speed of light. So quickly, in fact, that Jenna had wondered if they shouldn't be looking for someone involved with the media. But Sam kept remembering Elyssa's words. That the ghost mentioned the witchcraft trials and cults. That didn't necessarily mean modern-day pagans. But the well-publicized feud between the two most prominent covens could not be ignored.

Among the information Angela had sent was details on a legend. Sam had specifically asked about the Gullah culture and the boo-hag.

"Listen to this," he said, reading the information.

And he told them about an old folk story and a boy named Billie Bob who just could not find a wife. So his father fixed him up with the daughter of a swamp woman. He was stunned when he met her. She was gorgeous, with dark eyes, dark hair, and a beautiful body. She didn't want to be married by a priest, but was willing to stand before a judge. So they were married and she was the perfect wife by day. But at night she never came to bed. Suspecting the worst, Billie Bob, armed with sugar and honey and all manner of gifts, went to see a local conjuring woman. The old woman told him to pretend that he was asleep, then watch what his wife did. The next night Billie Bob did just that, following his wife up to the attic where she sat at a wheel and spun off her skin. All bloody muscle and bone, she headed out into the night. Billie Bob was terrified, so he went back to the old conjuring woman who told him he had to paint every window and door in the house blue, except for one. She also told him to splash salt and pepper on her discarded skin. He did both, and when she returned home, she found herself trapped, as the blue doors were a weakness. When she slipped back into her skin, the salt and pepper burned her horribly. In a panic, she crashed through an attic window and turned as bright as a falling star, her body exploding into chunks of flesh that were enjoyed by the swamp gators. Billie Bob was sad. The conjuring woman told him that he should not be. He'd had no wife, only a boo-hag. Once she'd tired of him, she would have brought him to her boo-daddy, who would have eaten his flesh, drank his blood, and gnawed at his bones.

"But Billie Bob didn't become chow," Sam said. "It's a bit like a vampire story, or even a story about our old concept of witches, bringing their new recruits to Satan. Their version of a boo-daddy."

"And what does a boo-hag have to do with Salem?" Martin asked.

"What about the Gullah culture up here?" Sam asked.

"We have a few transplants, but—"

A uniformed officer entered the room, escorting Devin and Rocky. Jenna rose to quickly hug and welcome the newcomers. As it turned out, Rocky knew Detective Gary Martin. They explained what had just happened.

"A second murder?" Rocky asked. "People are being killed in period costume. Not to profile anyone here, but—"

"We're looking for the head of the opposing Wiccan coven now," Martin made clear.

Rocky looked at Sam. "Divide and conquer? We've been reading the briefs on the murders all the way here."

"What do you mean 'divide and conquer?'" Martin asked.

"We'll go off and interview members of the opposing team," Devin explained. "The more of us talking to people in a more casual manner, the better."

"And you think—"

Rocky leaned forward, "Gary, these are our old haunting grounds. We've dealt with murder here before. Bad things, involving people we knew. Out on the streets, we can do a lot of good."

Martin nodded. "But I need to be in the loop on everything. I was planning on heading to the mortuary tonight. I want to keep an eye on the place now that it has reopened. Two people are dead either in or near that place. But John Bradbury was no Wiccan."

"No, but he supported Tandy Whitehall," Sam said.

"How did you know that?" Martin asked.

"From hanging out in a bar."

"We don't have any viable suspects," Sam said, "except for Tandy Whitehall. And that's just because she seems to have a motive. She might also have an alibi."

"And unless we get out on the street, we'll have no idea about anything," Rocky said. "Hey, this is Salem. And Salem at Samhain and

Halloween? That means hope."

"I'm pretty sure a little nook or hole-in-the-wall bar is where we'll find Tandy Whitehall," Jenna said. "Surrounded by those who'll protect her."

Martin seemed both indignant and worried. "And that could be bad. They could be armed with more than curses. Man kills his wife. Son-in-law kills father-in-law. Junkie kills for drugs. That's the usual things. But these people around here are fanatics. You don't think they'll turn this into a stand-off, do you?"

"This killer doesn't want to get caught," Devin said. "He, or she, or *they*. And as for my real thoughts, I can't help but think that it's not this Tandy Whitehall at all. It's too obvious. We have to be casual. Walk in like customers. Hey, I still own my great aunt Myna's cottage. I'm almost a real live local girl. And Rocky is from Marblehead. Let us do this our way. We'll find what we're looking for."

"I don't have a lot of choice, now do I?" Gary said, an edge in his voice alluding to the influence of the Krewe of Hunters agents. "I'll be watching things over at the mortuary. We'll keep in close contact."

"I'll hang out at the mortuary with Gary," Jenna said. "You guys handle the streets. How's that?"

Sam looked back at her, surprised and annoyed. He didn't like being away from her in Salem. But she was already up, ready to leave with Gary Martin. Sam stood as well, gently laying an arm on her shoulder.

She smiled at him. "I'll be fine."

He accepted that, just as he accepted who she was, what she did, how they were different, and how they were alike. He loved her. And part of that involved letting her be who she was. But there was still the matter of the boo-hag.

"Where are we meeting up? And when?" he asked.

"Last tour at the mortuary is midnight," Martin said. "We can do it then. The next two days promise to be long. The day before Halloween, then Halloween itself. We need to catch this killer quickly, before this goes any further."

* * * *

Apparently nothing stopped Halloween.

The Mayberry Mortuary was packed, the parking lot full. Jenna and

Martin arrived in a police car, uniformed officers everywhere. Two at the entry, two by the ticket booth, one man watching the parking lot.

"I can only imagine the overtime," Jenna said, looking around.

"We don't really have a choice. Salem's economy would be totally in the trash if we had to start closing down things like this. Winter is cold as a witch's tit! Whoops, sorry. I'm sure that's politically incorrect now. But you know what I mean. Christmas is great, New Years, Wiccan holidays, we get people then. Summer is a fantastic time with school kids and families. But we can't lose Halloween. A lot of the locals only survive the off months thanks to what they make at Halloween."

"So the overtime is worth it," Jenna said.

But she doubted this killer intended to strike in the same place twice.

Martin used his phone, checking in with headquarters. Jenna paused in the parking lot, staring out over the cemetery, toward the trees and the edge of the forest. She'd volunteered to come with Martin only because she wanted to get back to the cemetery. She wanted the ghost of John Bradbury to come to her. She also wanted to know why she'd seen a boohag heading into the trees moments before she found a woman hanged.

"Still no sign of Tandy Whitehall," Martin said, hanging up. "Your coworkers are out, and we have officers trying to reach her. But she's seen the news by now and has to know we're looking for her. Probably long gone. I'm going in to do a walk-through. You coming?"

"I'll hang out here for a bit. I want to watch some of the people coming and going. I'll be in soon."

He left and she headed over to the busy ticket booth. She saw Micah working, but no Naomi Hardy or Jeannette Mackey. A young woman she'd never seen before sat next to Micah.

"Everything going all right?" she asked, watching him hand out tickets that were available from a pre-sale online.

He looked over at her. "We're sold out. But people get in line for cancellations. We're always crazy, but tonight is extra rushed."

Jenna overheard whispers from the crowd, where some of the visitors were commenting on how they could go to the place where the man's corpse had been hanged.

"You're a creep, Joe," someone said.

"Come on, creepy is fun. Afterward, we can go in the woods and find where that other corpse was hanging. The witch. Yeah, man, they hanged a witch."

Jenna grimaced at the nonsense. "Best of luck," she told Micah, moving down the porch steps, smiling and excusing herself as she moved through the crowd. Her smile faded as she made her way to the cemetery. She hated not being truthful with Sam. She loved him so much. He'd gone through the FBI Academy just for her, becoming a crack shot and a proficient agent. True, he talked to ghosts, and it wasn't a bad thing to be a lawyer who could talk to the dead. He seemed to be really worried about the boo-hag.

She entered the cemetery.

Most ghosts didn't roam around, moaning. Ghosts stayed for a reason, mainly to tell the living what happened to them. She'd seen fathers stay for children, mothers for a family, and children in a sad attempt to ease the pain of their parents. She knew ghosts who'd remained for centuries, hoping to see that history was not repeated. And, yes, she'd met a few in cemeteries. But, usually, they preferred being elsewhere. Tonight, however, one was here, following her. She threaded a path through the tombstones, glancing back to see the glow from the mortuary through the trees. If any of the visitors decided to head into the woods tonight, they'd be in for a surprise. The crime scene from the murder earlier was roped off, two officers watching over it. Finally, she stopped, noting a death's-head on the stone at her feet.

She turned.

John Bradbury faced her, still attired in his Puritan dress.

"We're truly trying," she said to him. "Elyssa tried to repeat what you told her. But we're not sure we understand."

He seemed to waver for a moment, gathering strength. Then he managed a weak smile. "I knew you would come. I tried hard to get someone to see, someone to know. It's not easy. I knew about you from Lexington House."

Jenna nodded. "Tell me exactly what happened."

He was a tall, nice-looking man, big enough that it must not have been easy to get his neck into a noose.

"I was working. Checking the connections on some of our automated monsters, readjusting the props on the embalming tables. I don't know where they came from. I just had a sense that someone was behind me."

"When you say you don't know where *they* came from—did they enter from the house or from the delivery doors? Did you smell something? Was anyone wearing aftershave or cologne? Or as if they hadn't bathed? Did you see their hands or anything about them?"

"I felt like I was hit by a bulldozer. I was standing there, then suddenly someone was behind me. I was slammed against one of the props, then I felt the rope go around my neck. They pulled it tight fast. I was struggling with the noose, trying to get it off. Then I was off my feet, being dragged and jerked. I couldn't really see anything but black. I think they were in costumes. Maybe capes."

"Were they wearing masks?"

"I don't know. But I never saw their faces. I heard them. The one said something giving 'dimension to the witch trials' and the other said 'to shut up.' Then the one who'd spoken first said, 'he's going to tell someone what we were talking about. The Wiccans, the cultists, the weirdos.'"

"That was it?" Jenna asked.

John Bradbury nodded. "They jerked the rope, and my neck snapped. I died. Then I felt like I was drifting, looking on, and I saw people coming through the mortuary. I kept trying to speak, but I realized they didn't see or hear me." He paused, smiling wistfully. "I worked with Elyssa. She had a way about her that reminded me of my oldest daughter. But I also felt that she knew things that maybe even she didn't know she knew. I felt her coming near me. I reached out with my mind. And she must have listened. Everyone else was pretty much just walking by me. She seemed to hear me. So I spoke to her. I then managed to follow her home. But I couldn't connect with her until the following morning. That was strange. But it happened."

"I am so sorry," Jenna said. "We're looking for two killers. But, John, I need you to think. Were they men, women?"

"I don't know. They were whispering. But you mentioned smells. I remember that it seemed absurd, but it was like I smelled a forest. Flowery, like an autumn breeze."

"Anything else?" she asked quietly.

"I was strangling, dying. And the thing is . . . my kids. They have to know that I didn't do this to myself. That I would never have left them, no matter how bad things seemed to be."

Jenna reached out instinctively, but touched nothing but a chilly breath of air. "They'll know. I'll make sure. You do know there was another murder?"

He nodded. "Gloria Day. I didn't like her very much."

"Did she have a lot of enemies?"

"On Halloween night, for years, Tandy Whitehall has been throwing a big gala. Gloria arrives in town and lures away half of Tandy's business. Gloria and I knew one another. We were never friends. She was more a bitch than a witch."

He was quiet for a minute. Jenna allowed him the moment of thought. She wondered what she looked like, standing in the graveyard, talking to herself. A number of family tombs were strewn between her and the mortuary, which probably blocked the vision of anyone who might have casually looked this way. The entire scene was vintage Salem at Halloween, complete with the giant old Victorian house, covered with webs and scarecrows and monsters, caught in an eerie glow that barely reached the cemetery.

"Red," John Bradbury said.

She waited.

"You made me think about that night. What I was feeling and smelling and I suddenly thought about the color red."

Jenna heard Sam from earlier with his story of a boo-hag. A body stripped down to muscle, bone, and red blood.

"Does that mean something?" he asked.

"I followed someone in a red costume into the forest. A red costume beneath a black cape. Does that mean anything to you?"

"What you mean…" a new voice said, "is that you followed someone in red and black into the forest, then found Gloria Day, the wretched bitch witch dead?"

Jenna turned toward the new voice. Female.

"Really, John?" Gloria Day said. "Bitch witch? How rude. I'm dead, too, you know."

The new ghost joined the party, wearing the same Puritan garb in which she'd died, standing with them among the lichen-covered tombstones. She'd been an attractive woman with dark hair, light blue eyes, a heart-shaped face, and a charming smile.

Gloria looked at Jenna. "You will find out who did this to us. And so help me, dead or alive, Wiccan, Catholic, Buddhist, whatever, I'll curse them in a fiery realm of hell where they'll burn for all eternity."

Chapter 7

"Where would a popular Wiccan head to avoid detection and the press?" Devin pondered, linking arms with both Sam and Rocky.

"Did you know her?" Sam asked Devin.

Sam knew that Devin had not started out as an agent. She'd first been an author of children's books—all based on a witch. She'd grown up in Salem and returned when her Aunt Mina left her a cottage on the outskirts of town. She and Rocky had met when Rocky had come to Salem. The murders they'd solved had traced all the way back to the days when Rocky had been in high school.

When the dead had first spoken to him.

Sam was fond of them both and had been glad when they'd become part of the Krewe. All of them were New Englanders from approximately the same area, hard not to share a few local peculiarities. For one, they all had the tendency to overuse the word "wicked." To a Brit everything tended to be "brilliant." In New England, things were just "wicked."

"I'd say she's hiding in someone's house," Rocky suggested. "The cops have a list of all her followers, so they'll be going door to door."

"Which doesn't mean much. There are no warrants. She's not under arrest, only wanted for questioning," Sam said.

Rocky grinned. "Can't get the attorney out of the agent, huh?"

"Thing is, once we get a murderer, we'd like to see he or she locked up, not free on a technicality."

"I just wish we could find this woman," Rocky said.

"Angela just texted me," Devin said. "There's a little place near the end of the Salem Harbor Walk, owned by a Wiccan woman who is in a hive that's an offshoot of Tandy Whitehall's coven. It's called the

Goddess, serves a lot of Paleo foods, vegetarian offerings, homemade wine and beer. It's two blocks from Tandy Whitehall's house. Sounds like a place to start."

"Sound good to me," Sam said.

So far they'd managed to keep themselves out of the news. He and Jenna had been involved in the Lexington House case four years ago. It had been just a little more than a year since Devin and Rocky had met here to solve an old murder, which had been hard on Devin, since it had involved one of her old circles of friends. They needed to maintain their anonymity.

They headed down along the dark streets, avoiding revelers, costumed or not. Sam had loved Salem growing up. True, a lot had gone commercial. But the Peabody Essex museum was wonderful, teaching the history of fear and suspicion and distrust of one's neighbors and what those emotions could do to a community. The people who lived and worked here gave the place a pulse. And yet the old could still be found, along with the new. Quaint stood side by side with fun and the silly. So many restaurants had brought in excellent chefs. The House of the Seven Gables still stood, a testament to the past and a reminder that the past came alive through great literary works. Ships continued to ride high in the harbor, beneath the moon, the water seeming to stretch out forever.

Devin suddenly squeezed Sam's hand. "One way or the other, if we find Tandy or not, you need to tell Rocky and me what's going on with you and Jenna."

He looked at her with surprise. "We're good. We're great."

"You were acting a bit strange. You kept looking at her as if you're afraid you're never going to see her again."

Rocky nodded. "She's right." Then he paused and pointed. "There's our place. Rambling, with lots of rooms. Plenty of hiding places. Angela may be hundreds of miles away from here, but she can track like a bloodhound."

"Let's see what we find before we canonize her," Sam said, grinning.

The bar/restaurant was situated in a house where a plaque on the door informed them that it had been built in 1787. Plain dark wood on both the outside and inside. Booths offered hardwood benches, those along the wall with backs. Doors opened to additional rooms on either side of an oblong bar. Like everything else in Salem, it was decorated. No monsters here, though. Only pumpkins, Indian corn, and all manner of natural fall decoration. The place was busy, but not overcrowded, and a young hostess asked them if they'd like a booth or a table.

They opted for a table. Soon, they were sipping locally brewed brown beer with steaming bowls of chowder before them, listening to the snatches of conversations from those around them.

"Will the gala go on? I mean a woman is dead," a tall blonde at the bar said to her companion.

"Probably. There are sponsors, bands and tickets were sold. They can't cancel it," her male companion said.

"I heard this is a real Wiccan hangout," another girl said.

"Tourists," Rocky murmured, then he looked at Sam. "What's up with you?"

Sam hesitated, but these were his coworkers. They'd worked well together because they were straight with one another, even when it seemed ludicrous.

"Boo-hag," he said.

"What?" Devin asked, a frown furrowing her brow. "That's not like a redneck banshee or something, is it?"

"More like a vampire, a really creepy, ugly one," Sam said. "And we keep seeing one in particular. A boo-hag nearly threw itself on the car when we were driving into town. And Jenna saw one right before she found Gloria Day's body."

"You mean—someone costumed as one?" Devon asked.

Sam smiled. "Sure, what else. And I dreamed about one coming after Jenna. I couldn't get to her in time, and it was going to suck the life out of her. A dream, I know. But boo-hag keeps coming up, and it's bugging me."

"Where would one find a boo-hag in Salem?" Devin asked. "If we find someone in a boo-hag costume on the street, we can't just stop and search him."

"There's a community of Gullah people here who I want to check out tomorrow morning," Sam said.

"Gullah?" Rocky asked.

"It's a blend of different African and island cultures, along with a Creole mix. The culture originally stretched from the coastal areas of the Carolinas to Florida. Now, it seems, they're mostly in South Carolina. The boo-hag is one of the demons, I believe, in their storytelling. It's hideous, shedding its skin, answering only to a boo-daddy."

"Ah, yes," a female voice said.

Sam turned and saw a petite, attractive woman standing behind him dressed in black and wearing a beautiful gold pentagram. Her platinum blonde hair was short and curled around a thin, lovely face.

Tandy Whitehall.

"Young and lovely women meet unwary men," she said. "They seduce them and use them, and, when the time is right, take their husbands or young lovers to their boo-daddy. He consumes them, down to gnawing on their bones. Every society has its monsters. The boo-hag is a bad one." She glanced around the table and smiled, then shook Sam's hand. "Emily told me you three were here. Would you care to come into the back where we can talk in private?"

"Tandy?" Devin said.

"Devin Lyle. You know, I miss your Aunt Mina. She was an amazing friend."

She drifted away from the table. They followed. Which seemed expected. They'd wanted to find Tandy Whitehall.

And had done so.

* * * *

Jenna knew this was her best opportunity to find out the truth.

"The oddest thing is that I don't believe Tandy Whitehall had anything to do with this," Gloria Day's ghost said. "You have to realize that some of the argument between us was all for hype and promo. We go about things differently—*went* about things differently." She looked at John Bradbury. "This is really so unfair."

"Tell me about it. I had children."

"And I'd hoped to have them one day, too," she said. "You didn't like me a whole lot, John. So don't pretend that you do now."

"I didn't like your Wiccan kick against haunted houses," he said. "You, I hardly knew."

Gloria made a face at him. "I just tried haunting the place, but no one could see or hear me."

"Could you two focus on the problem at hand," Jenna said. "We're trying to figure out who killed you, and disprove that it was two suicides."

"Hard to hang yourself over a tree," Gloria said. "You need some help."

"It's like with your death they want us to know a murderer is at work," Jenna said. "That might be because the killers have realized John's death isn't going to be accepted as a suicide."

"Either that," John said, "or someone is going about recreating the deaths of those condemned to hang, and maybe even Giles Corey's death, too. This could get really bad."

"Do they want it to look like a Wiccan war? If so, they missed the debate somewhere along the line. John and Tandy Whitehall were close," Gloria said.

"Gloria, I need to know what happened to you," Jenna said. "You didn't drive yourself out here, somehow make your car disappear, then hang yourself.

She wasn't meaning to be cruel, but Gloria seemed the type who wanted things straight.

And she did.

Gloria arched a brow with a shade of humor and said, "I don't know what happened. I was in the shop, just straightening up, and some kind of a bag was suddenly over my head. I was suffocating and passed out. I came to feeling the roughness of a rope around my neck, then agony and darkness. And I was here. On the other side. I wandered out of the trees and was surrounded by gravestones. I saw the mortuary up on the hill and had no idea how I had gotten here. And then, of course, I realized. I was dead. And I've been trying ever since to find someone who could hear me."

"Any smells?" John asked her.

"What?" she asked, looking at him, a faint wrinkling forming above her brows.

"A smell, a feel, a sensation? Anything?"

"The trees. I remember the smell of trees. Something like a forest."

"I smelled the same thing," he said.

"Did either of you recognize the scent? From a store, a shop, either one of the big department store colognes, or anything more local?" Jenna asked.

"I know where something close can be bought," Gloria said after a minute. "A woodsy scent. At Tandy Whitehall's shop."

"You really think Tandy did this?" John protested. "I'm a big man, and even with a noose around my neck it would take more than a tiny woman like Tandy to take me down."

"We know from what you heard, John, that there were two killers," Jenna said.

"I don't believe Tandy did this to me. I really don't," Gloria said, looking at John. "We had our differences, but I respected her. No, I may be dead, but right is right, and I won't attack the woman, even if I am dead." She seemed to shake off her sadness and looked at Jenna with purpose. "But I know that scent, and it can be bought at Tandy's shop."

"Tandy has disappeared," Jenna said. "She's wanted for questioning. Would she have fled Salem?"

"Never," John and Gloria both said.

Jenna's phone buzzed and she glanced at it quickly.

Sam.

She answered and learned that John and Gloria were right. Tandy was still here, with Sam, Devin, and Rocky, and Sam's assessment was clear. *She's not our killer.* So everyone seemed in agreement, Tandy was innocent.

Jenna looked over at Gloria.

"I appreciate you finding my body," Gloria said. "I could have hung there a long time."

But it had been the boo-hag who led her. Had it intended for her to find Gloria?

She texted Sam.

Check Tandy's inventory. Find out who bought a woodsy scent that she sells. Find out about the Gullah community.

She finished her text and looked up.

"Someone is trying to make this look as if the Wiccans are evil," Gloria said. "As if the community should be hanging us again."

"Or trying to make it look like a feud," John added. "I was killed, so someone from the other camp had to die, too."

"What do either of you know about the Gullah community?"

"I know a number of folks who moved up here who are basically Gullah, but they don't really follow any special practices. There's one church in town that has a Southern twist, but it's basically Baptist. Most of them attend there. They're actually all great people," Gloria said. "Where do they fit in here?"

"I don't think they come into it at all. I think that boo-hag is being used."

"Boo-hag?" John murmured.

"Creepy, soul-sucking yucky demon," Gloria explained. "Gullah. Red. Woodsy. Mortuary."

"Red mortuary?" Jenna asked quickly.

"Maybe it's because you said boo-hag," Gloria said. "But I have an impression of red in my memory. For some reason, I seem to remember a whisper of the word mortuary."

Gloria paused and gazed across the graves to the mortuary on the hill.

John joined her, then glanced at his wrist and shrugged with an unhappy sigh. "I always wore a watch. But it stopped when I died. Go figure. Loyal watch, I guess."

"It's way past midnight," Gloria said. "The lines are gone and people are leaving. They try to have it all closed up by 2:00 A.M."

Jenna looked over at the mortuary, too, which appeared both dead and eerily alive, as if on a plain between the living and the dead. Haunting, opaque, sheathed in garish Halloween décor, in the moonlight it appeared decayed and faded.

Jenna was certain the answers she sought lay there.

"I'm going up there," she said. "Care to join me?"

* * * *

The back room at the bar/restaurant reminded Sam of an old brothel, especially the brocade cushions in gold and burgundy on the sofas and loveseats. Tandy served them an excellent herbal tea and talked about Gloria Day.

"I have to admit some of the bad feelings were jealousy. Every time I looked at her, I thought I should start singing *Memory*. But I actually liked her. We both managed to get people to ball-hop on Halloween, after the Sabbat on the Gallows Hill, of course. There was plenty here for everyone. So I want you to know that I'm not leaving town. I have no intention of running."

"Tandy," Sam said. "We need a list of people who wear, or have recently purchased a scent you make at your store. It's something woodsy, smells like a forest, that kind of thing."

She found her phone and tapped a message. "I'm getting it for you."

He leaned forward. "And what do you know about the Gullah community?"

"How did you even know we had a Gullah community?" Tandy asked, bemused. "They're usually in coastal South Carolina or Georgia."

"We heard there was a group here," Devin said.

"We do have a group here now. Almost a hundred," she said. "All good people. Some are more conventional; some have converted more or less to the Wiccan religion. They have their own language, a Creole similar to a Krio language spoken in what's now Sierra Leone. Their religion is based on Christianity, but includes a great deal of believing in the spirits of their ancestors. I buy a lot of merchandise from them to sell at the store. Beautiful, hand-crafted masks and totems, and jewelry."

"What about the boo-hag?" Sam asked.

Tandy smiled at that. "What about it?"

"It seems to be a popular costume."

"Wait here," Tandy said.

She rose and disappeared from the room, returning a moment later with a young woman, clad in black, wearing a beautifully crafted pentagram.

"Sissy, this is Special Agent Sam Hall, and Special Agents Lyle and Rockwood," Tandy said. "Meet Sissy McCormick. She's from Gullah country in South Carolina."

"Nice to meet you," Sissy said, joining their grouping by taking the chair Tandy had vacated. "My people are Gullah."

Sissy was striking, her skin coffee-colored, her eyes a soft blue. She had dark hair, queued at the nape of her neck, wearing a black cape over a long black skirt and tailored shirt.

"You've chosen to be Wiccan?" Devin asked.

Sissy nodded. "Something speaks to all of us, and not always what's in our heritage. But, basically, I follow the tenets of almost any creed. Be good to others, care for the elderly, sick, and injured, cherish all children, never offer violence. Be a good human being."

"Nice," Devin said. "Gullah is based on Christianity?"

"Of course, but so is voodoo," Sissy reminded her. "And look, many fundamentalists have caused tremendous harm to others in the name of traditional religions. Every faith out there has those who choose to take it too far, or read into it what isn't there."

"Or use it," Sam said. "Sissy, we're seeing a lot of boo-hag costumes, or at least one boo-hag costume, over and over again. The boo-hag is a Gullah demon, right?"

Sissy nodded. "Some manufacturer came up with that awful costume. Red latex to look like a fleshless body, a horrible demon face. My mother was so upset. She said it's just going to make people anti-Gullah. But it's just part of Halloween. People dress up as crazed movie characters. They know Freddy and Jason and all those fictional killers are just from movies. They'll know that a boo-hag is simply from legend, like a vampire or a werewolf. No true Gullah in this community would ever buy or wear such a costume."

"Here we go," Tandy said, slipping a pair of reading glasses from her pocket to stare at an incoming message on her phone.

Sam's phone rang. He didn't recognize the number, but it was local, so he answered. For a moment, there was nothing. Then he heard something like a snuffled tear.

"Sam?"

For a split second, he was confused.

Then he knew.

"Elyssa?"

He heard a sudden cry.

Then a whispered voice. "You want this one to live? Then get your wise-ass partner under control. All of you back down. Leave this alone. Let these murders go into the great cauldron of unsolved crimes. That is if you ever want to see this kid again. You back off, and she's free on November 1. You keep it up, she dies before Halloween."

Sam forced himself to remain calm, glancing at Rocky, who knew what the look meant. Trouble. So he worked to keep the caller on the phone, as Rocky called headquarters to run a trace through Sam's phone.

"We want Elyssa alive," he said. "But I have to have some kind of assurance that you're not going to hurt her regardless of what we do."

A soft laugh seeped through the speaker. "Trying to keep me on the line? You're on your cell, not at police headquarters. So you'll need some time to run a trace. It was nice that Elyssa kept this number in her phone. You were an attorney, so I would hope you understand the fine art of negotiation."

"So negotiate," Sam said. "I have to know that Elyssa remains alive."

"A call every six hours. But there'll be a new number each time. If I even suspect you're playing me, this pretty little girl will be hanged. Maybe by the witch memorials or the cemetery, right there amidst all the tourist attractions. Or I could find another cool place. So you need to find Jenna

Duffy. Actually, I wouldn't mind seeing her hanged either. Now there's a thought..."

"Touch her," he said, "and you'll face hell a thousand times here on earth before going to the real thing."

Laughter followed his remark.

Cocky? Why not? Two people were already dead.

"Sam," the voice said, "I'm disappointed in you. I thought you were a negotiator."

"Okay, let's negotiate and not threaten other people."

He looked at Rocky, who was listening to his own phone, watching Sam with anxious eyes. Rocky nodded. They had a location.

"Okay. I agree. Don't kill anyone else and we'll back off. I'll get Jenna right now, and she'll back off."

"Six hours, you'll get another call."

The line went dead.

Tandy Whitehall seemed oblivious to the tenor of the call. But Sam had risen and stepped back where only Rocky and Devin knew who'd been on the other end of the line. But he was now really interested in that scent from Tandy's shop.

"It's popular with a number of men in town," Tandy said. "And a few women. Here's the list one of my cashiers just sent me. John Bradbury bought that scent, and I guess he suggested it to a lot of his friends and coworkers."

Sam took the phone and looked at it.

"Mortuary? Now?" Rocky asked.

"You got it." And he handed the phone back to Tandy.

"I'll turn myself in to the police now," Tandy said.

"No. Sit tight, right here. You too, Sissy."

"The call came from the mortuary," Rocky said.

He hurried out the door, wondering just which one of the people on the list was now holding Elyssa Adair hostage there. He didn't want Tandy calling the police. Not until he found out exactly who he was dealing with, someone that might even now be stalking Jenna, who may be stumbling into a trap.

Chapter 8

The mortuary was definitely clearing out. People were leaving in groups and singles. The ticket booth was closed. By the time Jenna walked across the porch and reached the front door, no one was around, the last of the visitors having reached the parking lot. She entered through the front door and no costumed actor greeted her.

"Detective Martin," she shouted.

No answer.

"Micah? Jeannette? Naomi?"

No reply.

The silence gave her a sensation of unease, one that had nothing to do with the fact that she was accompanied by two bickering ghosts. She ignored them, allowing them to follow her as she searched the ground floor rooms, amazed that the actors and staff could clear out so quickly. Also, no one had locked up. She passed through the dining room with its array of skeletal guests. On through the kitchen, where it appeared that a massacre had taken place. Fake blood leaked from a cauldron on the stove top, body parts lay scattered on a table, but no actor-chef or cook standing around with a plastic butcher knife to put chills and thrills into the bloodstreams of attendees.

"Goodnight," she heard someone call from the front of the house. "Last one out, lock up."

Jenna hurried to the front door. But whichever performer had just left had done so quickly. She could just make out a dark form heading to the parking lot. She hustled back to the kitchen.

"There's no one down here," Gloria said, following close behind her.

"We should check upstairs," John suggested.

"We should go to the basement," Gloria said.

Jenna was irritated. "Stop. I'll go up first, then we'll go down."

The stairway up seemed misty in the eerie black lighting used for the haunted house attraction. She moved carefully, unnerved, not wanting to be taken by surprise. One by one, she searched through the second floor rooms. Spider webs, creepy creatures, all manner of frights remained. But no one person. Where the hell was Detective Gary Martin? She heard the sound of movement coming from the back of the house. She hurried across the hall to one of the rooms that looked down over the delivery entrance to the old embalming rooms.

"Basement," she said.

"Told you," Gloria whispered.

"Where is everyone?" John asked.

"Good question. Detective Martin should be here," Jenna said. "Let's see what's down in the basement."

She moved quickly, hurrying down the blackened stairs. Portraits adorned the walls that started off as depictions of the living and changed to rotting skeletons from different perspectives. She ignored them and hurried around to the stairs to the basement. Her phone rang. Sam. She hit the answer button.

John screamed.

She whirled to see why.

A fist came out of the darkness, smashing against the side of her face. Her body crashing down the rest of the stairs, her phone disappearing into the misty darkness of the embalming room below.

Before the world vanished, she heard Sam's voice through the phone. Calling her name.

* * * *

Sam spotted the mortuary, high on the hill, glowing opaque in the strange mix of moonlight and artificial electric haze. No cars filled the parking lot. The building seemed to be alive, its upstairs windows like soulless eyes. The front door appeared to be a gaping mouth caught in a strange and twisted oblong O of horror.

"Not sure how exactly we should be doing this," Rocky said.

"Maybe call the local police?" Devin murmured.

"No," Sam said. "We handle this ourselves."

The killer had threatened to kill Elyssa and now he probably had Jenna too. No time to wait for the locals.

"No police," he said.

And neither of his colleagues argued since, among those who bought the woodsy scent from Tandy Whitehall's shop was Detective Gary Martin. A cop gone bad? Sam didn't know. Especially since another man associated with the mortuary had purchased the scent, too.

The head of the paranormal research department.

Micah Aldridge.

* * * *

Jenna tumbled down the stairs, feeling every bruise to her body, but managed to roll out on the floor and draw her weapon.

She heard an eerie laugh.

"You have no idea how much trouble you're in," a voice told her in a hoarse, eerie whisper.

Then she heard another voice. Gloria Day. "It's a boo-hag."

Down the steps one came. But no demon. Instead, a living, breathing person in a boo-hag costume, armed with a Smith and Weston pistol gripped by red latex-clad hands.

"Stop," she commanded.

But the costumed person ignored her. "Throw down your gun. Now."

A snap of sound and a system was turned on that offered first eerie music, then the deep, rugged, masculine voice of the attraction's narrator. "And so Proctor died as well, for, as he was supposed to have said, the girls did, in the end, make devils of far too many a man and woman. It was in June of 1692 that the first of the condemned were hanged. Before it was over, nineteen would die in such a manner, and one man, Giles Corey, would be pressed to death."

A sudden flow of light sprang from one of the niches.

She heard a sob of fear and terror.

"Auntie Jenna? Help me. Please!"

Elyssa stood in the niche, supported on a stool, a noose around her neck, a second costumed boo-hag at her side ready to rip away the stool.

* * * *

Sam came through the mortuary front door. Rocky and Devin had slipped around the house, intent on entering the basement via the delivery entrance. He moved with care. What he wanted was to barge in with guns blazing and wrap his fingers around the throat of the killer now threatening Elyssa and Jenna. But he told himself to slow down, use caution. His head pounded, ready to explode. All he could hear was Elyssa's sobbing through Jenna's phone, from four minutes ago.

A lot could happen in four minutes.

He climbed the porch steps and saw that the mortuary's front door hung half ajar. He entered the foyer and looked around, certain from the acoustics and sounds made when he'd called her that the phone had dropped in the basement. He hurried through the garish decorations and around to the stairway.

A body lay on the floor right by the door to the basement stairs.

Not a prop.

Micah Aldridge.

He hunkered down and felt for a pulse. Faint. But there. He found his phone and dialed 911 requesting an ambulance and the police. He'd identified himself and asked for no sirens. His phone blinked for an incoming call. Rocky. He answered and told him the situation and that help was coming.

He left the fallen man and headed for Jenna and Elyssa.

Knowing now who he was about to encounter.

* * * *

"We'd been debating how to handle this, and honestly," the costumed boo-hag said, "you weren't on our original list. But that's okay. We had you running all over looking at Wiccans and talking about the Gullah people, and don't you love our costumes?"

Elyssa was still sobbing, but Jenna realized that struggling just caused the rope around the young girl's neck to chaff more. Elyssa's wrists and ankles were tied. Once the stool was kicked aside, there'd be no recourse for her.

"It's not that I care," the boo-hag said. "I really don't care if the kid—or you—live or die. You couldn't let a damned suicide be a suicide. You just had to turn it into a murder investigation."

"You're so sadly mistaken," Jenna said. "The medical examiner knew immediately that John Bradbury had been murdered."

The boo-hag by Elyssa spoke out angrily, "That's because your good buddy Sam Hall talked the medical examiner into believing that. It could have been left a mystery, accepted as a suicide. But that's all right. Eventually they would have blamed the Gullah people or the Wiccans. But you! Bursting in here, pushing everyone around. Here to pat poor baby cousin on the back. What made you start running around screaming murder anyway?"

"John Bradbury told Elyssa it was a murder and that you would murder more people. Then John found and told me about the way you two attacked him. And yes, you did have us investigating what might be going on in Salem. But this has nothing to do with the Gullah community or the Wiccans or history, except in whatever way you thought you could use it. This is all about greed."

John Bradbury's ghost floated over the niche where he'd been hanged, and where Elyssa was now dangerously close to meeting the same fate, swiping angrily at the air.

To Jenna's surprise, the boo-hag moved back, as if the movement had been felt.

"Don't you understand?" the boo-hag behind Jenna said. "We're in complete control. So I'll only say it one more time. Drop your gun or my pal over there will kick the stool out from under your cousin."

"I don't think so," a new voice suddenly announced.

Sam.

The boo-hag whirled around. "Sam Hall. The great attorney, P.I. No—great FBI special agent now. Have you forgotten all about our negotiation?" stairway boo-hag said.

"Not at all."

The boo-hag beside Elyssa said, "We've still got all the cards, Special Agent Hall. Come down here. Now. Or this girl dies."

Jenna recognized the woman's voice. Naomi Hardy. And she knew that their suspicions had been right. This had nothing to do with the past, nothing to do with feuds or beliefs. "Naomi Hardy. You did this for a promotion? You killed people—you probably planned on killing more people to create a real Wiccan war and send a Wiccan to prison—all for a promotion."

The boo-hag's head whipped around. "She knows who I am."

"Shut up," the boo-hag on the stairwell said.

"You know, I thought at first that it was either Micah—or even poor Detective Martin," Sam said. "But, Jeannette, you and Naomi have to be the two dumbest murderers I've ever met!"

Of course, Jenna thought. Jeannette Mackey.

"Kill the stupid girl, Naomi. Do it," Jeannette yelled.

"They'll shoot me," Naomi said.

Jenna thrust herself up and burst toward the niche, trying to get to Elyssa. She could make that move because Sam had her back. Luckily, Naomi Hardy stayed hesitant. The boo-hag on the stairwell raised her red latex arm to fire, but Sam slammed his arm down on hers and the weapon went cascading down the stairs.

Jeannette screamed in fury.

Sam and the boo-hag went down.

"Kill the damned girl," Jeannette roared.

Naomi recovered her wits and kicked the stool.

Jenna lunged forward to save her cousin. Arms around the girl, she supported her weight so the rope could not tighten around her neck. Naomi's body began to jerk from side to side, as if being pushed hard. Gloria Day and John Bradbury were trying to have an affect on her, but it was another ghost who managed to stop her. He was in Puritan garb as well, a big man, heavy-muscled, broad-shouldered. He appeared before Naomi, who gasped and backed away.

Rocky burst through the basement door and helped Jenna get the noose down and off from Elyssa's neck. Sam wrenched Naomi Hardy aside. Devin Lyle appeared and cuffed Naomi, telling her that she was under arrest.

Sirens screamed from outside.

Help was coming.

The reign of terror was over.

* * * *

"Naomi Hardy thought that she had a brilliant way to become the head of the company? Get rid of John Bradbury? In the midst of the highest paying time of the year? Really? She did this for a job?" Devin Lyle asked.

"It was a pretty damned good job, from what I understand," Sam told her. "And trust me, I didn't get it until the end. I knew that both

Detective Martin and Micah Aldridge had ordered that cologne—Scent of the Pine—Tandy Whitehall sold. And since both of our victims had smelled it, the scent seemed involved. But, as we would have learned had we had time to ask Micah about it, he bought it for Jeannette Mackey, who loved the scent."

They were all at Devin's place, a charming cottage on the outskirts of town. Devin had inherited the house from her Aunt Mina, who remained after death, still watching over Devin when she was in Salem. Mina was with them now, shaking her head over the terrible things an emotion like greed could cause a person to do. She'd done her best to make the ghosts of John Bradbury and Gloria Day comfortable in her house.

"How did she get Jeannette involved?" Rocky asked.

"Jeannette saw herself as a seer, a medium, the rightful agent at the gate. Their agreement was that once Naomi became boss, she'd find another place for the haunted house company to operate. They were so obsessed with what they wanted to do that they were willing to kill," Jenna said.

"And," Sam explained, "Jeannette knew all of the legends about the new local cultures and communities beyond the Wiccans. She also hated both Tandy Whitehall and Gloria Day. What better way to get back at the two women than kill the one and get the other arrested for her murder."

"They planned on killing more people," Elyssa said.

Her parents, overcome with gratitude for Jenna and Sam and the Krewe members, had allowed her to come along with the adults.

"Who was next?" Rocky asked.

"Somebody named Sissy," Elyssa told them. "In case they didn't blame the Wiccans, they'd start looking at the Gullah people. They never intended for any of us to survive the night."

"I'm pretty sure they thought they'd killed both Gary Martin and Micah Aldridge," Sam said.

Martin had been discovered in the basement, a bad gash to his head. But both men were going to be all right.

"Here's what I understand," Sam said. "They had to kill John and make it look like a suicide. They figured that it might not work, so they planned an elaborate scheme to kill more people and make it look like an inter-Salem cultural war of some kind."

The ghostly presence of Gloria Day said, "So I died because of you, John?"

"It seems so. I'm sorry."

"You didn't die because of John," Auntie Mina pointed out. "You died because of two greedy, sick, demented women."

"Who really thought they could kill me, Sam, and Elyssa, and get away with it," Jenna said. She looked at Sam and smiled. "Thank goodness they underestimated you."

"They underestimated the Krewe," Sam said.

"I don't think Jeannette cared if she died," Elyssa said. "As long as she took us with her. But, you're right. Thank goodness for the Krewe. I think I'd like to be part of this one day." Elyssa leapt to her feet. "Gotta go."

"Where?" Jenna asked her.

"Party. It's Halloween. And I'm rather an important person right now. My guy is here for me. Don't worry, my parents love Nate."

She kissed and hugged them all, thanking everyone profusely, and then she was gone.

"What about us, John?" Gloria asked him. "Shouldn't we be going somewhere by now? Into the light or whatever."

John looked at her. "I'm thinking about sticking around for a bit."

"How lovely," Aunt Mina said.

Gloria reached for John's hand. "If we're going to stick around together, we're going to play give and take. Come on. It's Samhain."

"Where are we going?"

"Gallows Hill, of course."

John Bradbury groaned, then shrugged and took Gloria's hand. "Why not."

They said their good-byes and disappeared.

"I'm curious about one thing still," Jenna said. "There was a third ghost there last night. A powerful ghost. He was in Puritan apparel, big guy, like a hearty farmer type. Then he was gone. Who was he? There's not another victim somewhere, is there?"

Rocky shook his head. "The two women spilled everything at the station. No more victims."

"Big dude, powerful, looked like a farmer?" Mina said. "Might have been John Proctor, sick to death of watching more horror over petty jealousy and greed. Those bitter human emotions might have caused the hysteria once, but he wouldn't want to see it happening again. Could have also been George Burroughs. He was a big dude, too."

"I wish we could thank him," Jenna said.

"I'm sure he feels thanked," Mina said.

"Are we going out for Halloween?" Sam asked.

Jenna jumped up laughing and grabbed his hand. "No. We're staying in. Rocky, Devin, Mina, thank you for your hospitality. We're going back to Sam's house. Uncle Jamie is busy dishing out Halloween treats. We're going to be alone for a while."

Sam jumped up, ready to comply, but noted, "We'll all head back to Krewe headquarters in the morning."

And he told them all goodnight. Outside, the moon had risen over a beautiful, brisk, October night.

Jenna rose on her toes and kissed his lips.

"Trick or treat?" he asked.

"I intend to see that on this Halloween, every move we make is going to be one hell of a treat." She drew a finger down his chest. "Here, there, and everywhere."

He kissed her.

"I shall strive to make this a happy, happy Halloween too."

They drove to his house, and then they were alone.

There were all manner of treats...

And it was a very happy Halloween indeed.

Sign up for the 1001 Dark Nights Newsletter
and be entered to win a Tiffany Key necklace.

There's a contest every month!

Go to www.1001DarkNights.com to subscribe.

As a bonus, all subscribers will receive a free
1001 Dark Nights story
The First Night
by Lexi Blake & M.J. Rose

Turn the page for a full list of the
1001 Dark Nights fabulous novellas...

1001 Dark Nights

WICKED WOLF by Carrie Ann Ryan
A Redwood Pack Novella

WHEN IRISH EYES ARE HAUNTING by Heather Graham
A Krewe of Hunters Novella

EASY WITH YOU by Kristen Proby
A With Me In Seattle Novella

MASTER OF FREEDOM by Cherise Sinclair
A Mountain Masters Novella

CARESS OF PLEASURE by Julie Kenner
A Dark Pleasures Novella

ADORED by Lexi Blake
A Masters and Mercenaries Novella

HADES by Larissa Ione
A Demonica Novella

RAVAGED by Elisabeth Naughton
An Eternal Guardians Novella

DREAM OF YOU by Jennifer L. Armentrout
A Wait For You Novella

STRIPPED DOWN by Lorelei James
A Blacktop Cowboys ® Novella

RAGE/KILLIAN by Alexandra Ivy/Laura Wright
Bayou Heat Novellas

DRAGON KING by Donna Grant
A Dark Kings Novella

PURE WICKED by Shayla Black
A Wicked Lovers Novella

HARD AS STEEL by Laura Kaye
A Hard Ink/Raven Riders Crossover

STROKE OF MIDNIGHT by Lara Adrian
A Midnight Breed Novella

ALL HALLOWS EVE by Heather Graham
A Krewe of Hunters Novella

KISS THE FLAME by Christopher Rice
A Desire Exchange Novella

DARING HER LOVE by Melissa Foster
A Bradens Novella

TEASED by Rebecca Zanetti
A Dark Protectors Novella

THE PROMISE OF SURRENDER by Liliana Hart
A MacKenzie Family Novella

FOREVER WICKED by Shayla Black
A Wicked Lovers Novella

CRIMSON TWILIGHT by Heather Graham
A Krewe of Hunters Novella

CAPTURED IN SURRENDER by Liliana Hart
A MacKenzie Family Novella

SILENT BITE: A SCANGUARDS WEDDING by Tina Folsom
A Scanguards Vampire Novella

DUNGEON GAMES by Lexi Blake
A Masters and Mercenaries Novella

AZAGOTH by Larissa Ione
A Demonica Novella

NEED YOU NOW by Lisa Renee Jones
A Shattered Promises Series Prelude

SHOW ME, BABY by Cherise Sinclair
A Masters of the Shadowlands Novella

ROPED IN by Lorelei James
A Blacktop Cowboys ® Novella

TEMPTED BY MIDNIGHT by Lara Adrian
A Midnight Breed Novella

THE FLAME by Christopher Rice
A Desire Exchange Novella

CARESS OF DARKNESS by Julie Kenner
A Dark Pleasures Novella

Also from Evil Eye Concepts:

TAME ME by J. Kenner
A Stark International Novella

THE SURRENDER GATE By Christopher Rice
A Desire Exchange Novel

SERVICING THE TARGET By Cherise Sinclair
A Masters of the Shadowlands Novel

When Irish Eyes Are Haunting
A Krewe of Hunters Novella
By Heather Graham
Now Available!

Devin Lyle and Craig Rockwell are back, this time to a haunted castle in Ireland where a banshee may have gone wild—or maybe there's a much more rational explanation—one that involves a disgruntled heir, murder, and mayhem, all with that sexy light touch Heather Graham has turned into her trademark style.

* * * *

Chapter One

"Ah, you can hear it in the wind, you can, the mournful cry of the banshee!" Gary Duffy—known as Gary the Ghost—exclaimed with wide eyes, his tone low, husky and haunting along with the sound of the crackling fire. "It's a cry so mournful and so deep, you can feel it down into your bones. Indeed. Some say she's the spirit of a woman long gone who's lost everyone dear in her life; some say she is one of the fairy folk. Some believe she is a death ghost, and come not to do ill, but to ease the way of the dying, those leaving this world to enter the next. However she is known, her cry is a warning that 'tis time for a man to put his affairs in order, and kiss his loved ones good-bye, before taking that final journey that is the fate of all men. And women," he added, looking around at his audience. "Ah, and believe me! At Castle Karney, she's moaned and cried many a time, many a time!"

Yes! Just recently, Devin Lyle thought.

Very recently.

Gary spoke well; he was an excellent storyteller, more of a performer than a guide. He had a light and beautiful brogue that seemed to enhance his words as well and an ability to speak with a deep tone that carried, yet still seemed to be something of a whisper.

All in the tour group were enthralled as they watched him—even the youngest children in the group were silent.

But then, beyond Gary's talents, the night—offering a nearly full moon and a strange, shimmering silver fog—lent itself to storytelling and ghostly yarns. As did the lovely and haunting location where Gary spun his tales.

The group sat around a campfire that burned in an ancient pit outside the great walls of Castle Karney, halfway between those walls and St. Patrick's of the Village—the equally ancient church of Karney, said to have been built soon after the death of Ireland's patron saint. A massive graveyard surrounded the church; the Celtic crosses, angels, cherubs, and more, seemed to glow softly in a surreal shade of pearl beneath the moon. That great orb itself was stunning, granting light and yet shrouded in the mist that shimmered over the graveyard, the castle walls, and down to embrace the fire itself—and Gary the Ghost—in surreal and hypnotic beauty.

Gary's tour was thorough.

They'd already visited the castle courtyard, the cliffs, the church, and the graveyard, learning history and legends along the way.

The fire pit they now gathered around had been used often in the centuries that came before—many an attacking lord or general had based his army here, just outside the walls. They had cooked here, burned tar here for assaults, and stood in the light and warmth of the blaze to stare at the castle walls and dream of breeching them.

The walls were over ten feet thick. An intrepid Karney—alive at the time of William the Conqueror—had seen to it that the family holding was shored up with brick and stone.

"The night is still now," Gary said, his voice low and rich. "But listen if you will when the wind races across the Irish Sea. And you'll hear the echo of her wail, on special nights, aye, the heart-wrenching cry of the banshee!"

Gary—Devin knew from her cousin, Kelly—was now the full-time historian, curator, and tour director at Castle Karney. She'd learned a lot from him, but, naturally, she'd known a lot already from family lore. Kelly Karney was her cousin and Devin had been to Castle Karney once before.

The Karney family had held title to the property since the time of St. Patrick. Despite bloodshed and wars, and multiple invasions first by Vikings and then British monarchs, they'd held tenaciously to the property. So tenaciously that fifteen years ago—to afford the massive property along with repairs and taxes—they had turned it into a fashionable bed and breakfast, touted far and wide on tourist sites as a true experience as well as a vacation.

Gary, with his wonderful ability to weave a tale, was part of the allure—as if staying in a castle with foundations and a great hall begun in the early part of the fifth century was not enough!

But Gary had gained fame in international guidebooks. While the Karney family had employed him first for the guests of the B&B, they'd always opened the tours to visitors who came to the village and stayed anywhere there—or just stopped by for the tour.

"Indeed! Here, where the great cliffs protected the lords of Karney from any assault by the Irish Sea, where the great walls stood tall against the slings, rams, arrows, and even canon of the enemy, the banshees wail is known to be heard. Throughout the years, 'twas heard each night before the death of the master of the house. Sometimes, they say, she cried to help an elderly lord make his way to the great castle in the sky. Yet she may cry for all, and has cast her mournful wail into the air for many a Karney, master or no. Saddest still, was the wailing of the banshee the night before the English knight, Sir Barry Martin, burst in to kidnap the Lady Brianna. He made his way through their primitive sewer lines of the day, thinking the castle would fall if he but held her, for she was a rare beauty and beloved of Declan, master of Karney Castle. Sir Martin made his way to the master's chambers, where he took the lady of the house, but Declan came upon him. Holding the Lady Brianna before Declan, Sir Martin slew her with his knife. In turn, Lord Declan rushed Sir Martin, and died himself upon the same knife—but not until he'd skewered Sir Martin through with his sword! It was a sad travesty of love and desire, for it was said Sir Martin coveted the Lady Brianna for himself, even as he swore to his men it was a way to breech the castle walls. While that left just a wee babe as heir, the castle stood, for Declan's mighty steward saw to it that the men fought on, rallying in their master's name. Aye, and when you hear the wind blow in now—like the high, crying wail of the banshee—they say you can see Brianna and her beloved. Karney's most famous ghosts are said to haunt the main tower. Through the years, they've been seen, Brianna and her Declan—separately, so they say, ever trying to reach one another and still stopped by the evil spirit of Sir Barry Martin!"

There was a gasp in the crowd. A pretty young woman turned to the young man at her side. "Oh! We're staying at Karney Castle!" she said. "And the main hall is just so hauntingly—haunted!"

"Ahha!" Gary said, smiling. "Hauntingly haunted! Aye, that it is!"

"We're staying there, too!" said an older woman.

"Ah, well, then, a number of you are lucky enough to be staying at the castle," Gary said. "Ten rooms and suites she lets out a night! Be sure to listen—and keep good watch. Maybe you'll see or hear a ghost—there are many more, of course. It's been a hard and vicious history, you know. Of course, you need not worry if ya be afraid of ghosts—while the main tower is most known to be haunted, Brianna tends to roam the halls of the second floor, and that's where only the family stays."

Devin felt a hand on her shoulder and heard a gentle whisper at her ear. "You, my love. Have you seen Brianna?"

It was Rocky—Craig Rockwell, the love of her life, seated by her side, their knees touching. And it was the kind of whisper that made her feel a sweet warmth sear through her, teasing her senses.

Rocky was her husband of three days.

But though she smiled, she didn't let the sensual tease streak as far as it might. Oddly enough, his question was serious; partially because they were staying in the old master's suite, since they were family, through marriage—Rocky, through her. Devin, because her mother's sister April had long ago married Seamus Karney, youngest brother of the Karney family.

His question was also partially serious because they were who they were themselves—and what they did for a living, rather strange work, really, because it was the kind that could never be left behind.

She and Rocky had been together since a bizarre series of murders in Salem. Devin owned a cottage there, inherited from a beloved great aunt. Rocky had grown up in nearby Marblehead and had—technically—been part of the case since he'd been in high school. As an adult, he'd also been part of the FBI—and then part of an elite unit within the FBI, the Krewe of Hunters.

Devin had been—and still was—a creator of children's books. But, she'd found herself part of the case as well, nearly a victim.

Somehow, in the midst of it all, they'd grown closer and closer—despite a somewhat hostile beginning. As they'd found their own lives in danger, they'd discovered that their natural physical attraction began to grow—and then they found they desperately loved one another and were, in many ways, a perfect match. Not perfect—nothing was perfect. But she loved Rocky and knew that he loved her with an equal passion and devotion.

That was, she thought, *as perfect as life could ever get.*

And, she'd discovered, she was a "just about as perfect as you were going to get" candidate for being a part of the Krewe as well. That had meant nearly half a year—pretty grueling for her, really—in the FBI Academy, but she'd come through and now she was very grateful.

Rocky had never told her what she should or shouldn't do. The choice had been hers, but she believed he was pleased with her position—it allowed them to work together, which was important since they traveled so much on cases. While the agency allowed marriages and relationships among employees, they usually had to be in different units. Not so with the Krewe. In the Krewe, relationships between agents aided in their pursuits.

While Devin had never known she'd wanted to be in law enforcement before the events in Salem, she felt now that she could never go back. She belonged in the Krewe because she did have a special talent—one shared by all those in the unit.

When they *chose* to be seen, she—like the others—had the ability to see the dead.

And speak with them.

It wasn't a talent she'd had since she'd been a child. It was one she had discovered when bodies had started piling up after she returned to live in Salem. The victim of a long ago persecution had found her, seeking help for those being murdered in the present in an age-old act of vengeance.

She still wrote her books, gaining ideas from her work. And being with the Krewe made her feel that she was using herself in the best way possible—helping those in need. She'd never wanted the world to be evil. And the world wasn't evil—just some people in it.

She did have to admit that her life had never seemed so complete. But, of course, that was mainly because she woke up each morning with Rocky at her side. And she knew that no matter how many years went by, she would love waking to his dark green eyes on her, even when his auburn hair grayed—or disappeared entirely. She loved Rocky—everything about him. He was one of the least self-conscious people she had ever met. He towered over her five-nine by a good six inches and was naturally lean but powerfully built, and yet totally oblivious to his appearance. Of course, he took his work very seriously and that meant time in a gym several days every week. Now, of course, she had to take to the gym every week herself.

Rocky was just much better at the discipline.

Better at every discipline, she thought dryly.

And also so compassionate, despite all that he'd seen in the world. When her cousin had called her nervously, begging her to come to Ireland, Rocky had been quick to tell Devin that yes, naturally, Adam Harrison and Jackson Crow—the founder and Director Special Agent of their unit, respectively—would give them leave to do so. And it had all worked out well, really, because they'd toyed with the idea of a wedding— neither wanted anything traditional, large, or extravagant—and they'd made some tentative plans, thinking they'd take time after and head for a destination like Bermuda.

They chose not to put off the wedding; in fact, they pushed it up a bit. And instead of Bermuda or the Caribbean, they headed to Ireland.

A working honeymoon might not be ideal. Still, they'd been living together for six months before they married, so it wasn't really what some saw as a traditional honeymoon anyway. And, St. Patrick's Day was March 17th, just three days away from their landing on the Emerald Isle that noon. Her cousin, Kelly Karney, had promised amazing festivities, despite the recent death of Kelly's uncle, Collum Karney—the real reason they had come.

A heart attack, plain and simple.

Then why was Collum discovered after the screeching, terrible howl of the banshee with the look of horror upon his face described by Brendan?

"They say," Gary the Ghost intoned, his voice rich and carrying across the fire, and yet low and husky as well, "that Castle Karney carries within her very stone the heart and blood of a people, the cries of their battles, the lament of those lost, indeed, the cry of dead and dying…and the banshee come to greet them. Ah, yes, she's proven herself secure. 'Castle Karney in Karney hands shall lie, 'til the moon goes dark by night and the banshee wails her last lament!' So said the brave Declan Karney, just as the steel of his enemy's blade struck his flesh!"

Devin turned to look up at the castle walls.

Castle Karney.

Covered in time, rugged as the cliffs she hugged, and... Even as Devin looked at the great walls, it seemed that a shadow fell over them to embrace them, embrace Karney. A chill settled over her as she looked into the night, blinking. The shadow as dark and forbidding as the...

As the grave.

As Gary said, as old as time, and the caress of the banshee herself.

Welcome to Storm, Texas, where passion runs hot, desire runs deep, and secrets have the power to destroy...

Nestled among rolling hills and painted with vibrant wildflowers, the bucolic town of Storm, Texas, seems like nothing short of perfection.

But there are secrets beneath the facade. Dark secrets. Powerful secrets. The kind that can destroy lives and tear families apart. The kind that can cut through a town like a tempest, leaving jealousy and destruction in its wake, along with shattered hopes and broken dreams. All it takes is one little thing to shatter that polish.

Reading like an on-going drama in the tradition of classic day and night-time soap operas like *Dallas*, *Dynasty*, and *All My Children*, *Rising Storm* is full of scandal, deceit, romance, passion, and secrets.

With 1001 Dark Nights as the "producer," Julie Kenner and Dee Davis use a television model with each week building on the last to create a storyline that fulfills the promise of a drama-filled soap opera. Joining Kenner and Davis in the "writer's room" is an incredible group of *New York Times* bestselling authors such as Lexi Blake, Elisabeth Naughton, Jennifer Probst, Larissa Ione, Rebecca Zanetti and Lisa Mondello who have brought their vision of Storm to life.

A serial soap opera containing eight episodes in season one, the season premiere of *Rising Storm*, TEMPEST RISING, debuts September 24th with each subsequent episode releasing consecutively this fall.

So get ready. The storm is coming.

Experience Rising Storm Here... http://risingstormbooks.com